Colorstruck

By Mia Sanders

Typesetting by FormattingExperts.com

Contents

PART 1: JONATHAN

PART 2: DAX

Dedications

I thank God for being my Rock, for always protecting me and bringing me this far! Without Him, nothing is possible.

My parents and sis: Love you so much! Your support and unconditional love get me through each day.

A special thank-you to J'Nan Kirby McManaman for the title Colorstruck! I never would have thought of it on my own, and it fits the storyline so well. Love it!

Thank you, Formatting Experts, Ann Proyous, and Kyle Courtright! You all are so awesome, putting up with my procrastination (I'm working on it!), indecisiveness, and struggle with organization. Thanks for hanging in there!

Trice Hickman, you're the best book coach and mentor anyone could ask for. Proud of you for all of your accomplishments, as well. Thanks for all you've done to help me along this journey.

Amy Knupp, thanks for the cutesy notes you put in the margins while editing, and for helping to make this book mistake- free! You're so awesome.

Bruce, you inspire me. Thanks for getting me to delve deeper into my psyche, to think outside of the box.

Mike, thank you so much for your creative input!

Once again, there are so many who have assisted with my work. Beckie, Amanda, Mimi, Jaime ... the list goes on!! Grammie! Grandpa! Paul!

Oh my goodness. Think I'll write a book strictly to thank everyone!

xoxo
Mia

PART 1:

JONATHAN

Chapter 1

"We're closed," the store employee said, his blue eyes narrowed as he looked at her.

Brushing a stray curl off her forehead, Patience McKlendon glanced at her watch.

"But I thought you stayed open till nine. It's only seven thirty."

The owner shrugged. "I just decided to leave early tonight."

He stood motionless behind the register of the furniture store, his eyes never leaving her face. They were the only two in the place on that warm, August night in Dallas, Texas. The *tick, tick, ticking* sounds coming from a grandfather clock in the corner were magnified in the otherwise quiet atmosphere. Couches, coffee tables, and ceiling fans surrounded them as they stood facing each other. The lighting was dim, and the air conditioning must have been on sixty degrees. Although extremely hot-natured, Patience shivered, partly from the cold temperature but also from his intimidating presence. The man appeared to be in his late forties, tall, with broad shoulders and muscles that threatened to burst through his shirt. He should have been working at a gym or rescuing large animals from danger, *not* managing a furniture place. She guessed his height to be at least six feet, two inches, and his weight was definitely over two hundred pounds. His black hair was very short, in a crew cut.

Cocking her head to the side, Patience glanced at his name tag and then looked up at him almost shyly.

"Oh, okay, Pete. Sorry about that. I'll just come back tomorrow."

"We're not open on Sundays," he replied sharply, his deep voice commanding respect. Although the words he said were matter-of-fact, they were tinged with rudeness.

Squaring his shoulders, Pete cleared his throat and began cleaning off the cluttered counter in front of him. Receipts, staplers, scissors, and notepads had been thrown haphazardly around the register like a tiny tornado had hit. Patience watched as he organized the items, pondering what to do next. This was *the* best, and most reasonably priced, furniture store for miles. She'd purchased her king-size bed here three years ago, and also found duplicates of two lamps her dog, Rory, had broken last month. It was then that she'd spotted and fallen in love with a dining room table that was on sale.

Out of all the times she'd shopped here, Patience had never met this man Pete, who obviously owned the store, for it was Pete's Furniture. He wasn't the most charming person, or even attentive. Yet all of the other employees had been super friendly and helpful. She thought about leaving and driving twenty miles to another store, or shopping online. But truth be told, she was lazy when it came to shopping. Plus, she had to have this particular table. It was gorgeous.

"Hmm, if I remember correctly, the sign outside indicates you're open on weekends."

"Nope, just Saturdays," he replied, never looking up.

Patience's green eyes grew wide, as the stray curl fell back down onto her forehead. She couldn't believe this. The customer was always right, in her opinion. And in this case, the sign was always right. She took a step forward, just inches away from the register. She pulled her purse higher up on her shoulder, then winced from pain as the strap got tangled in her long, curly hair. To anyone else, the move would have been endearing. But Patience rolled her eyes, annoyed at herself for being clumsy. She was a complete klutz, always tripping over the curb or bumping into things.

She freed the honey-colored strands from her purse, turning her attention back to the owner.

"Sir, if you would just allow me to purchase that dining room table over there"- she gestured with her head to the back of the store- "I'll quickly be on my way."

A tiny voice in the back of her head whispered, *just let it go.* She tried to dismiss the uneasiness she felt in the pit of her stomach. Having always been a people person, friendly to everyone and personable, Patience couldn't understand why this man was being so difficult.

She smiled again, trying to lighten the mood. Despite the chilly temperature, beads of perspiration began to trickle down her back. She knew it was out of nervousness.

To her dismay, Pete exhaled loudly, slamming the stapler down with a *thud* on the counter. He purposely strode to the front of the store, yanked the sign off the door with such force it made her jump, and hastily flipped it over to the word *Closed*. Glancing over his shoulder at her, as if to make sure she didn't miss the message, he clipped the sign back onto the door for the public to see. Turning on his heel, he walked toward the counter, a scowl on his face.

"Now," he began, his blue eyes narrowed into tiny slits, "what part of *we are closed* do you not understand?"

Patience took a step backward, a chill running down her spine. Never before had she been on the receiving end of such animosity from a stranger. She could almost feel the invisible daggers being thrown by him. She was apprehensive about pressing the issue. After all, they were the only two in the store. Furniture really wasn't that important. Yes, it was time for her to leave.

* * *

As she exited Pete's furniture, Patience wondered why the owner hadn't locked the door before she'd come. He said the store was closed, after all. But she was no fool. A lousy dining room table wasn't worth all this hassle. Plus, Pete had looked as if he were ready to strangle her when she'd started asking a bunch of questions. He wasn't playing around. And if he *had* killed her, there would have been no witnesses.

I'd be the star of Unsolved Mysteries, she thought with a shudder.

Glancing around the near-empty parking lot, she toyed with the idea of shopping for a while. The furniture store happened to be located in the middle of an outdoor mall. There were a few small items she needed, including a blow-dryer and toaster. She giggled as a passerby tripped over an empty water bottle on the sidewalk. He quickly looked around to see if anyone had noticed. A warm breeze ruffled Patience's untamed curls; she searched her purse for a ponytail holder.

Unbeknownst to her, she looked stunning standing there. Her thin, five-foot-nine-inch body definitely set her apart from the others. Her caramel skin tone, moist with sweat at the moment, was the envy of her best friend, Jana, who had dark brown skin. Her green eyes seemed to sparkle whenever she became excited or passionate about something. And her wild mane, which was the color of honey, only added to her exotic good looks. Sharise, her African-American mother, kept her own hair very short and chemically straightened. Otherwise it would be an Afro, which was not an option for her. She worked as a financial manager for a bank and said the dress code was strict. And that included hairstyles, tattoos, and so on. Two years ago, Sharise had sported a' fro and was immediately sent home.

"That's racist!" John, her Caucasian father, had exploded after hearing about it that night.

Her mother disagreed. She had sided with the company, who found the hairstyle "distracting" to customers. Sharise didn't like the negative attention she received whenever she wore her hair in braids or natural. She'd shared with them some of the comments people made that weren't so flattering, to say the least. But to her daughter, she was gorgeous. Patience had been as angry as her father after hearing about Sharise's employer. Although they were living in the twenty-first century, some still held on to ancient beliefs. She didn't go as far as John, calling them racists, but it still angered her that they'd sent her mom home for such a silly reason.

John had put an arm around the two women affectionately, pulling them close in a group hug.

"I'm the luckiest man alive. I have the best-looking wife and daughter in the world! But that also makes me the *unluckiest*. I never get any sleep at night. Anyone messes with either of you, he's dead, plain and simple!"

The *most* beautiful thing about Patience, however, was that she didn't realize she was attractive. People flocked to her wherever she went, whether it was the grocery store, bank, a concert, or football game. And it didn't matter if she wore jeans with a tank or an elegant dress. She also abhorred makeup, which was too expensive and took too much time to apply, in her opinion. Besides, she didn't need it. It amazed her how many times a stranger would approach her while pumping gas, giving her his or her phone number. Yes, she even attracted some females out there. Men and women alike stumbled over puddles of drool in her presence. And she was friendly to everyone. She never cut someone off, exclaiming she was too busy to chat. Her parents complained she could get into trouble that way, but she didn't care. She tried to treat people the way she wanted to be treated.

She walked toward her car, thankful she'd found a close parking space. She needed to pat her face dry with a Kleenex before continuing to shop. It was embarrassing to feel her shirt stuck to her back from sweat. Having grown up in Texas, she thought she'd be used to the extreme heat and humidity by now. But at the age of twenty-five, she doubted it would ever happen. She did not see relief on the horizon.

Grabbing a handful of tissues, Patience locked the car door before she could change her mind. As she made her way back to the sidewalk, she noticed two women tapping on the door to Pete's Furniture. Both appeared to be in their late fifties and were dressed warm and somewhat sophisticated. One even wore a scarf around her neck, and although night had fallen, Patience was sure the temperature was still ninety degrees. She almost fainted from imagined heat-stroke at the sight of their clothing.

The two women peered inside the store. One tugged at the handle on the door, which was locked. However, the other lady pointed at the ceiling inside, apparently noticing the lights were on. They chatted for a bit, each looking extremely irritated. One had her arms folded across her chest, while the other checked the time on her watch. A few minutes later, the store owner appeared, turned the sign over to where it read *Open,* and unlocked the door.

He let the women in with a smile.

She couldn't believe her eyes. She stood a few feet away, temporarily paralyzed from shock. Pete, who had practically pushed her out of his place, welcomed the other customers with open arms.

Maybe he has a twin, she thought sarcastically, her lips pressed in a thin line. Anger began to creep inside her body as she realized Pete was prejudiced. He had refused to sell furniture to her yet let the Caucasian women in, probably without a second thought. She pulled the strap of her purse higher on her shoulder, her gaze fixed on Pete's Furniture. Her hand on the doorknob, she paused for only a moment. She watched through the glass as the women browsed, chatting while Pete tidied up the place.

Taking a deep breath, Patience knew what she had to do.

Cautiously, she opened the door and stepped inside. Her heart pounded furiously in her chest. She'd never liked confrontation. Usually she just let things go, not wanting to hurt others' feelings. Or it would take her fifteen minutes to summon the courage to tell a person no, or maybe. However, this was important. It had to do with equal rights.

Pete had begun texting but looked up when he heard her come in. His face went from pale to beet red in a matter of seconds. Their eyes met, and for a moment, just one tiny moment, time seemed to stand still. She overheard the two women talking excitedly about the same dining room table she'd been interested in. Not knowing what else to do, she stood there by the entrance, seething inside.

He cleared his throat, obviously uncomfortable with the present situation. He opened his mouth to speak and then closed it again.

She made her way to the counter, squaring her shoulders and holding her head up high. She was determined not to show the uncertainty she felt.

"So," she began in a shaky voice, "you decided to reopen the store." It was a statement, yet her tone made it sound like a question.

He shrugged. "Yes."

"Great," she responded flatly. Searching through her purse, she found her checkbook and a pen. "When can I expect the dining room table over there to be delivered?"

Clearing his throat again, Pete glanced at the other customers who were approaching the register. The first one spoke up.

"Sir, *we* are interested in purchasing the table."

Patience could feel butterflies fluttering in her stomach. Raising her chin a bit higher, she spoke up.

"I saw it first, therefore it's mine."

The first woman stood her ground. "How could you see it first if you came in *after* us?" She was about a foot shorter than Patience but looked tougher and meaner. Actually, she resembled a bull-dog in many ways, with her broad shoulders and crinkly forehead. Her white hair framed her face dramatically, gargantuan and frizzy.

"Actually, I spotted the furniture last month. I just returned tonight to buy it."

The woman's friend said nothing, listening to the sharp exchange of words. Patience couldn't believe she was going through this much trouble for a table Rory would probably destroy in two weeks.

Pete turned to her suddenly. "Isn't there anything else in the store you find ... appealing?"

She shook her head.

"No." It was a single word, yet it held so much power.

"Are you sure?" he pressed.

"Yes, I am positive."

He gestured grandly with his arm toward the middle of the store.

"We have a dining room set over there, and if you don't like ivory, I can order it in any color you wish. I'll even give it to you for fifty percent off."

"Nuh uh."

Patience could tell he was beginning to feel bad, but she also sensed he was afraid of disappointing the other customers. He probably would have given her anything else in the store free of charge had she just run along like a good little black girl. She briefly thought of her uncle Clarence, her mom's brother. His friends called him Pookie. He lived in Forney, which was about twenty-five miles from Dallas. But he visited often, claiming Patience was his favorite niece. And she adored him. The two had a lot in common, other than the fact that he thought the world was against him.

Clarence had extremely dark brown skin and had been the victim of much ridicule growing up. Kids constantly teased him about his complexion, and sadly, the emotional scars hadn't healed. Now, at the age of forty, he had a huge chip on his shoulder. He was always accusing someone of being prejudiced. If a hostess wanted to seat him at the back of the restaurant, she was a racist. If the mechanic was too busy to fit Clarence in for an oil change, he didn't like black people. He loved Patience's father, John, and he also had a best friend who was white, but other than that, he didn't get along very well with Caucasians.

Patience, on the other hand, was slightly naïve when it came to race and society as a whole. She believed most people were tolerant of other cultures and races. Whenever someone mistreated her, she didn't automatically come to the conclusion that he was a racist. Maybe he was rude to everyone. Maybe he was having a bad day. There were so many possibilities for people's behavior. And she chose to have an open mind until a person flat-out told her he didn't like blacks.

A couple of years ago, she had run into some closed-minded individuals when dating. Sam, her first serious boyfriend she'd fallen for, had parents who didn't like African-Americans. But with his blond hair, blue eyes, and fair skin, he had taken a chance by dating her. He'd adored her. Yet in the end, he had chosen his family over her. And she didn't blame him.

Pete sighed loudly, bringing Patience back to the present.

"What if I throw in a gift card?"

The Caucasian women exchanged knowing looks.

Patience wasn't letting him off that easily. Truth be told, she didn't want the table anymore; it would have held bad memories of this incident. Plus, it was the principle. This closed-minded man needed to know it was not okay to treat people this way. The color of one's skin shouldn't matter. At least in her eyes, it didn't.

Clenching her fists at her sides, she felt her heart rate quicken.

"Do not patronize me. You can keep the damn table. However, I'm sure the Better Business Bureau would love to hear about my dreadful shopping experience," she finished, a smirk replacing the frown on her lips.

She turned on her heel to leave, but not before witnessing his mouth drop open and his eyes grow wide. As she made her way to the door, another person entered the store. She waited for Pete to tell the man they were closed, yet he didn't. The customer appeared to be in his late thirties and was tall and lean, with thick blonde hair and blue eyes. He held the door for her as she exited.

"Young lady!" Pete yelled after her, but in the blink of an eye, Patience was gone.

Chapter 2

Patience coughed as smoke filled her spacious kitchen the next morning. She'd decided to try out a new recipe for a breakfast casserole she'd seen on television. It had seemed easy enough when the chef had placed croutons at the bottom of a dish, sprinkling them with melted butter. Her mouth had watered as she'd watched him combine eggs, cheese, and pieces of fried bacon. He'd then poured the heavily seasoned batter over the croutons, placed it in the oven, and allowed it to bake for forty minutes.

Unfortunately, she never made it past the frying of the bacon. She'd placed the meat in the pan but gotten distracted shortly after, daydreaming about one of her ex-boyfriends.

Quickly, she turned on the overhead vent, tears running down her flushed cheeks. She darted across the room to open a window, tripping over her black lab, Rory. Patience winced as he yelped loudly.

"I'm so sorry!" she choked the words out, bumping into the refrigerator door she'd left open.

"Ugh!"

It frustrated her to no end that she'd become so clumsy lately. Her toe was still sore from stubbing it the night before.

She was always bumping into walls or falling over the coffee table. And poor Rory! She was shocked she hadn't killed him by now. It was obvious he felt that way, too. He used to sleep at the foot of her bed. Now he slept in the living room.

As she scrubbed the inside of the skillet, she once again allowed her mind to drift off. She thought of Roman, a guy she'd dated over a year ago.

The two had met when her dog had been hit by a car. Roman was a vet technician who had helped Rory after the accident. He'd driven Rory to the vet's office and had been so nice to Patience, explaining everything to her as she'd freaked out that horrible day. As it turned out, Rory's leg had been broken, but Roman had called her the day after the incident, checking on her beloved pet.

The attraction between Patience and Roman had been instant, and they'd found out they had a lot in common. Both were close to their families, both loved animals and children, and more important, the two were open-minded about race. In the past, she had encountered problems with the families of the men she'd dated. Sam and Tripp, who were Caucasian, had had a difficult time convincing their parents to accept her. Tripp had been willing to fight tooth and nail for their relationship, but it was Patience who had broken things off. She'd never wanted to be the cause of a division in a family.

Surprisingly, she hadn't been accepted by her African-American boyfriend's mother, either. Carolyn Peterson had told her she didn't approve of interracial dating or marriage. And like Sam, Jason had decided blood was thicker than water. He hadn't agreed with his mother's views, but he hadn't thought Patience was worth the conflict, either.

Needless to say, she had been ecstatic to finally find love that was colorblind. Roman had immediately introduced her to his family *and* friends, proudly displaying her to the world. She'd gotten along so well with his sisters, cousins ... the list went on. And everyone had adored the green-eyed, curly-haired beauty. All except his best friend, James, who'd believed races shouldn't mix. However, his disapproval hadn't affected their relationship in the least. Roman had even proposed after dating her only a few short months. Her best friends, Jana and Cole, had been less than thrilled, but she didn't care. She'd accepted.

Patience sighed, the sound of Rory's barking bringing her back to the present. She rinsed the sparkling clean pan off, placing it in the dishwasher for an extra wash. She brushed a tear from her cheek, as memories of her ex tugged her heart painfully. He'd been perfect, or so she'd thought at the time. Gorgeous, his dark brown skin had been flawless, and his smile could light up a room. Tall and muscular, he could have easily been a model for *GQ*. His best characteristics had been his sense of humor and ambition. He had been training to be a veterinarian.

The only problem? He'd been cheating on her their entire relationship. She'd gone to the gym one day and overheard two women talking about him and his friends. And with names like Roman, Maverick, and Heath, she had known she wasn't jumping to conclusions. The two had been complaining about how all men were dogs, and one said she refused to be the other woman. She had sat behind them, stunned for a moment, before leaving the gym to confront him.

Sadly, it had been true. Roman confessed that, although

he did love her, he also cared deeply for Michelle, the girl at the gym. James had introduced the two at a party the year before he'd met Patience. He'd dated Michelle for a while, the two broke up briefly, and that's when he'd fallen for Patience. Michelle had called him a couple months later, begging to get back together. He was torn.

"I think I'm in love with both of you," he'd choked out, tears flowing freely down his cheeks.

She hadn't believed she could survive the heartache. She was certain the pain would never go away. In the months following their breakup, she'd sworn off men forever. Each day, she threw herself into her work as a high school English teacher, and her evenings were devoted to Rory. Weekends were spent with her family and friends. She attended a baptist Church on Sunday mornings, which helped lessen the intense feelings of depression she was experiencing.

Rory continued to bark, the volume so loud Patience was positive the neighbors could hear. She wove her way through the still-smoky kitchen, past her living room, and into the foyer where Rory was. Funny, she hadn't heard the doorbell, but the poor dog continued to jump up and down, scratching and clawing at the door. Similar to the people in horror movies, Patience slowly opened the door without looking through the peephole. She'd often wondered why, when they heard a noise outside, the soon-to-be-victims just followed the sound, no gun, knife, or even broom in their hands.

There were children playing hopscotch on the sidewalk across the street, and a black cat ran through Patience's yard, picking up the pace when he caught sight of Rory. Her next-door neighbor, Ronny, was checking his mail. He wore only a bathrobe and, catching sight of her, immediately tightened the belt around the waist. He grinned sheepishly, waving at her as he walked quickly back to the privacy of his home. She giggled, her own face turning red on his behalf.

He had lived next door to her for only a year, but she felt as if she'd known him forever. The fifty-year-old doctor had moved from Chicago and, much to her surprise, was single with no children. He was a nice man, very attractive, and smart. He also had a great sense of humor, making her sides hurt at times with his senseless jokes and sarcastic comments. When they'd first met, he'd commented on her attractiveness almost immediately.

"I *know* you're mixed with *something*. Look at your hair. Your eyes! Your face! What are you? Half white, half Mexican? Italian?"

She laughed, shaking her head dramatically. "My dad is white and- "

"Your mama is black," Ronny finished for her.

"Yep."

He nodded his head. "Yes, you're right."

She laughed again. "It's good to know that I'm correct about my race."

Ronny folded his arms across his chest. "Let me ask you something. Being biracial, do you catch as much flak as we African-Americans do from society?"

"I'm sure I do."

His eyes searched her face, frown lines creasing his forehead. "I don't know, my dear. As a dark-skinned black man, I may have to respectfully disagree. I probably encounter more racism on a daily basis than you."

And so the debate began. Ronny, much like her friend Jana and Uncle Pookie, thought lighter-skinned minorities had an easier time in life than their darker brothers and sisters. In her opinion, Patience felt *all* minorities experienced some form of prejudice or racism sometimes. A person who didn't like blacks wasn't going to think, *well, she's okay because her skin tone is the color of caramel*. And the Ku Klux Klan wouldn't sit there trying to figure out if a person's mother was white, and then decide not to hurt her if she was. But Ronny was insistent that his dark skin and full lips hindered his ability to be treated fairly by everyone.

As he put it, "Whether I have a stethoscope around my neck or not, most people can't get past the color of my skin."

* * *

That afternoon, Patience sat in Chili's with Jana, scarfing down her favorite entrée, baby back ribs.

"You are so weird, Patience. Who in the world orders ribs with no sauce?"

"Jana! Will you please stay on the topic we're talking about?"

Jana took a huge bite of her chocolate molten cake, closing her eyes with pleasure.

"Mmmm."

Patience laughed. "Well, at least I don't always order dessert first."

Her friend shrugged. "Doesn't everyone do this?"

The two burst into a fit of giggles. The restaurant was packed that Saturday afternoon; they'd had to wait an hour to be seated. But neither one cared. It was the best place to catch up, hang out, and pig out. Every time one of them suggested trying a new place, they always ended up at Chili's. The waiters were hot, the food was delicious, and the atmosphere lively. Patience swore if she ever quit teaching, she'd apply there. Her friends usually rolled their eyes, claiming she was overqualified to wait tables.

"Then I'll advertise for them," was her usual response.

"Can I get you ladies anything?" Their server appeared from out of nowhere, it seemed. He'd been by their table at least fifteen times to check on them. Jana swore up and down he had a crush on Patience.

"We're good, but thank you ... again," Jana answered.

He grinned sheepishly, turned on his heel, and left. Patience leaned forward, resting her elbows on the table.

"I think he likes *you*, my friend."

Jana laughed. "No way! He can't take his eyes off you. See?" She gestured toward the kitchen area and, sure enough, their waiter was staring at Patience. When he noticed them looking at him, he brushed imaginary lint off his shoulder.

Jana smiled. "Wow, he's even cuter than Greg." Greg was her boyfriend-of-the-moment.

Patience took another bite of rib. "Can we please get back on the subject of Pete's Furniture? I swear that man was prejudiced. He refused to do business with me. He didn't like me because I'm black."

"You're biracial."

Patience rolled her eyes. "I *know*. But to him I'm just black."

Taking a sip of her soda, Jana nodded. "Yes, you're probably right about that."

"So what do you think I should do?"

"Call the NAACP and The National Action Network. Oh, and you also need to call John Wiley Price."

Patience scowled. "I'm serious."

"So am I."

"Part of me does want to contact the BBB and file a complaint."

"Then do it."

"However . . ."

Jana signaled for the waiter, who was hovering nearby.

"Aha! I knew it. You're not going to do anything. You're too nice. In the back of your mind, even though that man was a butthead, you wouldn't want him to lose his job over something like this. So you'll complain to me for a few weeks. And then you'll just let it go. I know you like a book." She asked for a to-go box for her entrée, waiting for Patience's response.

"Oh, you better believe I'm taking action. Racism is a serious matter. There's no way I'm ignoring this."

Patience took the check from their server. Her eyes widened when she noticed his name, phone number, and the words *Call me* scribbled at the bottom.

* * *

Jonathan.

Patience reached for the Chili's receipt the next morning, which she'd thrown haphazardly onto her dresser before going to bed the night before. She stared at the tiny, wrinkled piece of paper that had been stuffed into the pocket of her jeans. She smiled, remembering how Jana had given her a hard time the entire drive home after lunch, singing, "Patience has a boyfriend" at every stoplight. Her friend was notorious for teasing. She'd been that way ever since they were kids.

So his name was Jonathan.

She smiled. She'd always liked that name. It reminded her of a boy she'd had a crush on back in grade school. He was sweet, always staring at her in class with this silly grin on his thin face. Once, he'd rescued her from a tiny lizard that had escaped another child's backpack. The teacher had been as afraid as the children, standing on a chair as all havoc broke loose. Children screamed, running in every direction as Mr. Lizard made himself comfortable on Patience's desk. But brave Jonathan scooped him up in a flash, and Mrs. Jameson escorted them down the hall to set him free.

Opening her closet, she pondered what to wear to church. She considered the black slacks she wore every other Sunday and then decided against them. Some of the older ladies in the congregation frowned upon women wearing pants, and she wanted to blend in with the crowd today. She had no time to be worried about why others were staring at her that morning. She needed to concentrate on praying for Pete. He had been on her mind quite a bit, and after wrestling with her thoughts, she'd decided to give the situation to God. She just couldn't handle the stress alone.

It was tough for her to wrap her mind around the fact that some people didn't like her because of the color of her skin. If someone met her and thought she was too perky, fine. If they didn't want to be around her because she smiled too much, had bad breath, was too outgoing, or was afraid of her dog, so be it. If they preferred the company of introverts, wonderful. But she just could not imagine refusing service to someone simply because of the fact that he or she had brown, red, yellow, or white skin. And as a high school teacher, she treated all her students equally.

Patience chose a simple, mid-length sundress her mother had given her three months ago. The two had gone shopping for a baby shower and ended up in the women's department. She loathed shopping, but Sharise had bribed her with the promise of Mexican food afterward. The mother and daughter couldn't have been more different. Sharise loved cooking, shopping, and anything else girly. Patience, on the other hand, liked sports, reading, and being creative. She shied away from makeup, high heels, and attending weddings. Her mother couldn't believe that she was really her child sometimes.

Standing in front of the full-length mirror, she frowned. Sure, the lavender dress looked great against her skin tone, and fortunately, her hair had decided to behave today. It was pulled back in a high ponytail, making her look five years younger. No pimples had surfaced overnight, and she wasn't sweating. Even Rory seemed to approve, lying at the foot of her bed watching her quietly, his head tilted to one side curiously.

Yet there was sadness deep within her. The sparkle had dimmed in her eyes. Her shoulders sagged slightly, as a huge weight had been placed upon them. She couldn't erase from her mind the horrible treatment she'd received at the furniture store. The discrimination had been so blatant, so obvious. Usually people tried to hide their prejudice, at least in her past experiences. She was certain that some of the individuals she'd dealt with in the past hadn't liked her, but at least they'd pasted on fake smiles and pretended to tolerate her.

Glancing at the clock, Patience grabbed her sandals and purse, sprinted down the hall toward the kitchen, and flung open the pantry. She reached for a granola bar, knocking over the box of Cheerios that had been teetering on the edge of the shelf. Luckily it was closed. She searched for her car keys, finding them ten minutes later on the kitchen floor next to Rory's water bowl.

As she dashed out the door, Bible in hand, all she could think about was Pete.

Chapter 3

"Ugh! I do not feel like going to work tomorrow. Mondays are so hard. The kids are always lethargic, sitting with their heads down on the desks or staring out the window with a dazed expression. And usually only one or two have done their homework. The time creeps by, let me tell you."

Patience lay across her bed that night, gazing at the dark ceiling as she spoke to her mom on her cell. The two called each other at least ten times a week, possibly more. They were extremely close, and many thought they were sisters or best friends instead of mother and daughter. As an only child, she had been spoiled while growing up in the McKlendon household, both with love and money. John and Sharise called her their little cherub, swearing up and down that God had answered their prayers when she was born. They'd had trouble conceiving, yet when doctors told them they were both perfectly healthy, her parents hadn't given up. Five years later, their newborn daughter was smiling up at them in the hospital. John named her Patience because they'd waited so long for her to come into their lives.

Sharise laughed. "Darling, teenagers are like that. They

have no interest in school, church, or any other place that takes them away from their video games and cell phones."

"But, Mom, do you know how irritating it is to ask a question only to be met with dead silence?"

"Yep, I sure do! You were a teenager once."

The two laughed, and Patience rolled over to her side. Her clock read ten thirty, and she still had to grade a few more quizzes before the morning. She also had to return Cole's call. He'd left a message earlier that they needed to catch up. He was her best friend from childhood.

The two had met in elementary school when he'd dumped a bucket of sand in her hair on the playground. It had taken Sharise two days to get it all out. Cole's mother had come over that evening to apologize, and they'd all become fast friends. Patience and Cole had been inseparable ever since. In many ways, they were even closer than she and Jana. There was a bond between them that no one could explain.

In high school, she had hung out with him almost every day. Their friends and families constantly made predictions that the two would begin dating and end up married. And what a stunning couple they'd make. With Cole's dark hair and eyes, olive skin tone, and Cuban good looks, he and Patience made heads turn wherever they went. Both were close to their families. Both had taught at the local high school and loved children. Both were smart and creative. And after all these years, the two could talk for hours about anything, or simply sit together in silence, enjoying the other's company.

Yet there was nothing romantic between them. Sure, she could see how attractive he was, and vice versa. But it would be too weird to actually date him. He knew her inside and out, like a brother or a cousin. He'd been there for her through thick and thin, when she was sick with food poisoning and strep throat, and had held her hand through her first heartbreak. And she'd been there for him, as well, waiting on him hand and foot when he'd broken his leg playing football, pulling an all-nighter with him cramming for an exam he hadn't prepared for, and attending the prom as his date when she hadn't wanted to go. Yes, Patience and Cole were the best of friends, but nothing more.

Stifling a yawn, she let Sharise go, rolled out of bed, and gathered the quiz papers and her red ink pen. She stood in the middle of the bedroom for a minute, her ADD beginning to kick in. Rory watched as she grabbed the bottled water off her nightstand, taking a huge gulp of the lukewarm drink. Next, she set the papers back down and dressed for bed. She then opened the blinds, looking for who knows what out the window. All she could see was darkness. She pondered calling Cole but didn't feel like talking that late. He loved long phone conversations, so she knew he'd keep her until three or four o'clock in the morning. Wondering if she'd locked the front door, she ran to check. Finally, after promising herself she'd wake up early to grade the papers, she hopped into bed, drifting peacefully off to sleep.

* * *

The week flew by for Patience. Finishing up a month's worth of lesson plans, conducting two parent-teacher meetings- yes, she was already having trouble with two of her students- finally going to a dentist appointment she'd been putting off for a year, and taking Rory to a specialty pet-training class two evenings that week. He'd graduated from obedience school two years before, but basically the company had just taken her money. Rory had come out acting a bit worse than when he'd begun. Now, not only did he chew up her favorite shoes and the edge of her coffee table, he also dug holes in the backyard. The trouble with him was that he was so darn cute. And lovable. Anytime he did something naughty, he hung his head low, gazing up at Patience with those huge brown eyes, looking pitiful. Or he would lick her to death, knowing she was a sucker for nice dogs. He really was a sweet animal.

Friday evening, she decided to treat herself to ice cream and a trip to the bookstore. One of her all-time passions was reading, and she'd just finished *Look Again*, a mystery by one of her favorite authors, Lisa Scottoline. She couldn't wait to get her hands on her newest novel *Don't Go*. Plus, she wanted some new bookmarks and a romance to delve into. She could lose herself in a bookstore, inhaling the mouthwatering scents of lattes and cappuccinos that floated in from the coffee shop that was attached. She loved the atmosphere, quiet but not *too* quiet, with the occasional sound of a child giggling or a page being turned. Oftentimes, she'd go by herself so she could actually relax and not worry about someone tugging on her arm, asking every couple of seconds, "You ready?"

Cole was the worst person to accompany her. With all their similarities, it was hard for Patience to believe her best friend didn't like books. To him, reading was boring, and he usually insisted they just wait until the movie came out and see it then. Whenever she asked him to come with her to look for a new novel, he spent the first thirty minutes in the coffee shop, instructing her to meet him at the cash register when she was done. But of course, she would just be getting comfortable after an hour, which only irritated him. She smiled as she remembered how he would pace up and down the aisles, stopping every now and again to ask if she was done. Then he'd stand behind her as she read the sleeve of a book, breathing down her neck.

Her mother was no better, complaining the entire time that she was either hungry or would rather be shopping for clothes. And it never failed. Jana would always be really sweet in the beginning, offering to go with her and keep her company. Yet after a while, her friend became antsy, whispering questions like,

"How many books do you think they have in here?,"

"Why don't they have an African-American Author section?,"

"Why is it so quiet in here?," and

"I only see one black employee. And he's working in the back. What do you make of that?"

It was pretty safe to say that all of her friends and family drove her nuts, so it was better to go alone.

Patience stood in the self-help section, her purse on the carpet next to her feet, her eyes scanning the shelves for nothing in particular. She liked reading books that taught her how to set healthy boundaries with people, or basically how to just be a better person. She was so nice, and some individuals took advantage of that. Normally, she didn't regret helping others or lending a supportive ear to a grieving friend, but sometimes, when she gave an inch, people took a mile. She spotted *Boundaries*, which was propped up in front of her, but she'd read it.

As she bent down to browse the books on the middle shelf, her wild hair falling forward over her shoulders, she noticed someone pass the aisle she was on, back up, and walk by again. It was the same person who had passed by four or five times before. Ordinarily, she wouldn't have been paying attention, but his or her lime-green sneakers had caught her eye. As she returned to an upright position, a voice behind her said softly,

"You shouldn't set your purse down in public. Anyone could come and snatch it."

She whipped around, her eyes wide with surprise. It was the guy with the green sneakers. She laughed.

"If anyone grabs my purse, he or she will be very disappointed. I may have four dollars in it. Maybe."

He smiled. "Four dollars is a lot of money."

She knelt down, retrieving her purse and Lisa Scottoline's new novel.

"Yes, I guess it is. I could buy three tacos with that!" The two laughed again, standing across from each other awkwardly. There wasn't much space between them, as the aisles were narrow.

"You look familiar," she said, her head tilted to one side.

The guy smiled, his green eyes shining. "I'm Jonathan Brown. From Chili's."

"Oh, of course! You were our waiter last Saturday! How are you?"

"I'm doing excellent, now that I've run into you." His eyes twinkled behind his eyeglasses.

Patience blushed. Apparently Jonathan was not an introvert. First, he'd stared her down at Chili's and given her his phone number. Now he was acting openly flirtatious. She did her best to make eye contact, but he was standing extremely close, his gaze never leaving her face. She wasn't shy, by any means. However, his obvious interest made her slightly nervous.

"Oh?" she responded meekly, her cheeks still tinged with pink.

"Mmhmm. My day has been mundane, boring even. But tonight . . . "

She could feel her palms begin to sweat, and she held her breath as she waited for him to continue. There was no one else on the aisle, just the two of them. She had to admit, she liked the way it felt, being the object of this guy's attention. A blind man could see that he was attracted to her. And with his green eyes, light brown skin, and curly hair, the feeling was mutual. Yes, he could be described as handsome. He actually looked a lot like Patience. She wondered briefly if he was biracial.

"What are you thinking?" His words broke into her thoughts.

She smiled. "Nothing."

Jonathan dug into his pocket, pulling out a tiny piece of paper. He asked her if she had a pen. She dug around in her purse, finally finding an eyeliner pencil she never used. Her mother had given it to her a year ago with the hopes of turning her into a girly girl.

He laughed when she handed him the makeup. He grabbed a book from the shelf behind him, using it to set the blank paper on, and proceeded to scribble his name and number down. Again.

"Do you always carry small pieces of paper around with you?"

He grinned. "Yes, I do. I wanted to be prepared in case I ran into you."

"Seriously?"

Taking a step toward her, he reached up to brush the stray curl from her forehead.

"I've been trying to muster up the courage to talk to you for six months. Every time you come in to the restaurant, though, you're either with a guy or a group of people. The times you've come in alone, I've been too busy to swing by your table or felt intimidated."

"Why?"

He shrugged. "To be honest, I'm not sure. You're so beautiful, yet you also seem really friendly and approachable. So I don't know why." He handed her his number, and she promised to call.

"Well, I guess I better go pay for this," Patience said softly, pressing the book tightly against her chest. She was flattered by his words. Not since Roman had a guy shown this much interest in her. And Jonathan seemed sweet and very outgoing. She liked him already. Pulling her purse higher on her shoulder, she smiled broadly, her green eyes sparkling. And with a final wave, she headed toward the register.

Chapter 4

Patience accomplished quite a bit the next day. She woke up at five a.m. to take Rory for a nice, long jog along their favorite trail. It was conveniently located a couple of miles away from her home. They loved running. She'd taken Rory there ever since he was a puppy. It was such a relaxing place to hang out and people watch, feed the birds, and of course, to jog. It was *the* best form of exercise, according to her, mainly because she loved the outdoors. Breathing in the fresh air, taking in the beautiful surroundings, and clearing her mind of any problems she may be experiencing at the moment.

After returning home and showering, she decided to run errands. She stopped by the pet store to get more treats and toys for Rory, went to the car wash, and made a quick run to the grocery. On the way home, she dropped in on her parents, who only lived five minutes away. They always complained that she didn't visit enough. Later that afternoon, she worked on her first novel, *Which One?*, for nearly two hours. Ever since she was a teen, writing had been a hobby of hers, and she'd promised herself that one day she would begin to take it seriously. She loved teaching, but she also wanted to become an author.

Her ringing cell gave Patience an excuse to take a break.

"Hello?"

"Hey, it's Jana."

"What's up?"

"I can't talk but a second. Just wanted to let you know I gave Jonathan your number."

"You did *what*?"

"Yep, I sure did. Greg and I ran into him at Target earlier. He was asking all about you and said he gave you his number twice, but you haven't called. So . . ."

"So . . ." Patience mimicked.

Jana sighed. "Since you're being old-fashioned, he can now call you."

"I can't believe this. I was going to call him." Patience began pacing up and down the hallway. She bit her lower lip nervously.

"Look, we both know you had no intentions of making the first move. So now the ball is in his court. And trust me, he *will* call. I swear there were stars in his eyes as he talked about you."

The two friends talked a little while longer. Patience made up an excuse to let Jana go, as she needed some time to collect her thoughts. She also wanted to veg out in front of the television. She'd rented a couple of romantic comedies that morning and couldn't wait to unwind. It had been a busy week, and all she wanted to do was lose herself in the movies while chomping on microwave popcorn and Raisinets. She didn't care if the snacks were unhealthy. At least she had gone jogging that morning.

Patience dabbed her eyes with a Kleenex. It never failed-

The Notebook with Ryan Gossling always made her cry. She had seen the movie at least twenty times. She could even say the lines along with the characters. But still . . . it affected her every time. She loved tearjerkers, yet every once in a while, a good mystery caught her attention.

Although the DVD had ended ten minutes ago, she sat cross-legged on the couch, lost in thought. Rory lay by the coffee table, content after eating all the crumbs she'd dropped. The living room was dark, as it was seven o'clock in the evening and the only light came from the television. She wondered if she should call Cole or Jana. Perhaps she should make plans to actually do something. It *was* Saturday night, after all. But no, laziness overtook her body. If someone offered her a million dollars, she would not be able to get off the sofa.

As if reading her mind, the cell phone rang. She yawned, feeling all around for it in the dark. Finally, she spotted it on the carpet next to Rory.

"Hello?"

"Hi, is this Patience?" a male voice asked.

"Yes." She smiled, her heart suddenly doing a little flip-flop in her chest.

"This is Jonathan. How are you?"

"I'm doing great! What're you up to?"

"Oh, nothing, just patting myself on the back for gathering the courage to call you."

She giggled.

"I'm actually being serious. Since you never called me, I had to take matters into my own hands."

She sat up on the couch, staring blankly at the bookshelf against the wall. It was filled with books of all genres except horror. Once, she'd purchased a James Patterson novel, only to be scared out of her mind by the second chapter. She'd exchanged it the following day for something a little less … frightening. He was an excellent author, *too* good, in her opinion. Jana loved him and had seen all his movies, but Patience was a wimp when it came to those types of books.

"For what it's worth, I'm thrilled you called. Sorry I never reached out to you."

"It's okay. I think it's the man's job to make the first move, anyway."

She smiled. "Then why did you give me your number?"

"I have no idea."

The two wound up talking for an hour. Jonathan was hilarious, making Patience laugh with his dry humor and sarcastic comments. She found out he was twenty-three years old and lived in Plano, a city near Dallas. He was in his fourth year at UT Dallas, studying psychology. He planned on transferring to Baylor the following year for graduate school.

"How long does it take to become a psychologist?"

He exhaled dramatically. "Forever."

The two laughed.

"It'll take four or five more years, depending on the course load I choose to take on each semester. I want to eventually get into UT Southwestern for their postdoctoral training program. See, after high school, I decided to go ahead and continue, although my parents thought it'd be a good idea to take a year off. They were worried that I may get burned out, as I tend to take on too many projects at a time. Been that way my whole life. I have a huge work ethic and like to get things done as quickly as I can. Also, I was afraid I wouldn't want to go back if I took time to find myself. So here I am, working at Chili's part time, attending the university part time, and partying full time."

"*You're* a partier?" He didn't look like one to her.

He hesitated, choosing his words carefully. "I enjoy going out with friends."

She didn't respond.

"Does that bother you?" he asked.

"Oh, no, not at all. You just seem so . . . "

"Nerdy?" he finished for her.

"I wouldn't say that. But you do look smart. How about if I say you're a handsome bookworm?"

He chuckled. "Thanks for the compliment. I think."

They chatted a few more minutes when Jonathan suddenly took her by surprise with his next comment.

"Well, I guess I'll let you go. You probably have a date tonight."

Patience shook her head. "No."

"You do now."

She smiled. "Wow! You're not shy, are you?"

"No, I'm not."

The two made plans to meet at Brew, a popular coffee shop in Dallas. Tripp, whom she'd dated, worked there, and she briefly wondered if she would run into him. He had been pissed when she'd broken things off, but she was adamant. She'd wanted to remain friends, but he had nearly chopped her head off when she'd suggested it.

Suddenly catching her second wind, she hopped off the couch to begin prepping for her date. At least she *assumed* it was a date. However, he wasn't picking her up, and he'd asked at the last minute. According to the books she'd read on dating, the signs were definitely pointing to this just being a casual meeting. But the butterflies in her tummy and the wide, silly grin on her face told her it *was* a date. She was excited, no doubt about it.

Chapter 5

Jonathan took a sip of his vanilla latte, his eyes fixed on Patience.

"Looking for someone?"

She focused her gaze back on him, blushing slightly.

"No, why?"

"Every couple of seconds, you either glance over your shoulder or stare at the employees behind the counter."

She shrugged her shoulders, slightly embarrassed. "I'm sorry. I have ADD."

Leaning forward slightly, he raised an eyebrow.

"You do?"

She couldn't meet his gaze because she wasn't being completely honest. Instead, she studied the tiny packets of sugar at the end of their table.

"Yep."

When Patience had arrived at Brew twenty minutes before, she'd pulled into the nearly-deserted parking lot with a touch of anxiety. Almost subconsciously, she'd searched for Tripp's car, certain that he still worked there. She'd spotted Jonathan standing near the front door of the coffee shop, tall and handsome, his hands buried in the pockets of his jeans, exuding confidence without appearing arrogant. The navy blue Polo shirt looked great on him.

She'd hopped out of the car and walked toward him quickly, her wild curls tamed momentarily with an elastic band and her sundress complementing her slim figure. She had no idea how pretty she looked and didn't notice heads turn as she and Jonathan entered Brew. They made an attractive pair. Yet, in an almost sick way, they resembled each other enough to be siblings.

She took a small bite of her pumpkin bread, chewing slowly as she considered Jonathan's words. He was correct. She had been looking for someone. If Tripp did still work there, and if he happened to catch sight of her tonight, she didn't know what would happen. He had a temper and wasn't known for being tactful. He would barge up to their table and give her a piece of his mind, probably asking why she chose Brew as a place to bring a date. She wondered that herself as she sat there.

"Are you okay?"

Patience nodded, forcing herself to snap out of her walk down memory lane. It was rude to sit and think about a previous boyfriend while out with someone new.

She smiled. "I'm wonderful, thanks."

He smiled broadly. "Yes, you are."

The two began opening up then, talking about their families and friends.

"I have one sister, Lily, who's six years younger than me. She's a senior at Plano East, and even with the huge age gap between us, we're very close." He spoke with pride as he talked about her.

"She plays sports, all kinds, and has gotten straight As since kindergarten."

Patience laughed. "I didn't know they graded you in kindergarten!"

He laughed as well. "Of course they do!"

"Tell me about your parents. Are you close to them?" she asked, sounding a bit like Oprah.

He smiled. "Yes, we are extremely tight. My parents would do anything for us. They raised Lily to be a strong, independent young woman and me to have a high sense of self-worth and to believe I can do anything I set my mind to do. My mom is a doctor and Dad is an attorney, but they're very down-to-earth and easy to talk to."

She played with her napkin while listening.

"That's awesome. You and I are both lucky to have supportive, loving parents."

"Do you have any siblings?" he asked, his focus on her as if she were the only person in the room. As a matter of fact, he was one of the most attentive people she'd ever met, always nodding and making great eye contact. Even when someone passed their table, he appeared not to notice.

"Nope, I'm an only child. There are pros and cons, of course. I'm spoiled and can be a brat if I don't get my way sometimes." She winked and Jonathan whistled.

"Uh oh, I don't know if I'm brave enough to get involved with an only child."

She giggled. "Who says we're getting involved?"

He folded his arms across his chest, leaning back in his seat.

"If you're lucky, I may decide to ask you out again. Perhaps I'll even call you tomorrow."

51

Patience took a long drink of her bottled water. Although she loved the smell of coffee, she didn't particularly like the taste. Cole thought it was hilarious that she enjoyed Brew but usually ordered water or juice. She sat up straighter in her chair, her smile displaying perfectly straight, white teeth. He leaned forward across their table, taking her hand in his and giving it a gentle squeeze. His playful expression turned serious for a moment.

"All kidding aside, I like hanging out with you. If I were to call tomorrow, would you answer?"

"Yes."

"And if I happened to ask for a second date, would you say yes?"

"Mmhmm."

He kissed her hand lightly, and they sat quietly for a while, neither one wanting the night to end. It was Jonathan who finally broke the silence.

"Okay, time for a quick question and answer game so I can get to know you better."

"That sounds like fun."

"What's your favorite movie?"

"*Imitation of Life*," she answered without hesitation.

"Music?"

She smiled. "Hip hop and alternative."

"Mine, too. Color?"

"Purple."

"Food?"

"Mexican."

He grinned. "Same here! Television show?"

"*The Twilight Zone*."

His mouth dropped open in amazement. "This is so weird. I love that show!"

Patience shot him a quizzical look. "Are you just saying that so you can be like me?"

"Not at all. I am not kidding. We have a lot in common, it seems. Here, why don't you ask me the questions, then, since you don't believe we have the same likes?"

"That's a great idea," she responded playfully. "What's your favorite sport?"

"Football."

"Drink?"

"Chocolate milk."

She raised an eyebrow. "Activity to unwind?"

He nodded. "Reading."

There was a brief pause, and then she admitted,

"Those happen to be my favorites, too."

He ran a hand through his curly hair. "See what I mean? It feels pretty weird, sort of like we're in an episode of *The Twilight Zone*."

Rolling her eyes, she asked, "What's your *second* favorite food?"

"Chinese."

"Aha! Chinese food isn't even on my list. So that's one difference we have."

He pretended to be hurt. "And that pleases you? I'm kind of sad about it."

"Well, I am relieved. It was beginning to freak me out a bit. First, we look alike. And second, all the things we like to do, eat, and participate in match. Bizarre."

"We look alike?"

53

She nodded. "Yes!"

He laughed. "You're right. I hope we're not related." He watched her, examining her face carefully.

"What are you thinking?" she asked, taking the last bite of bread and savoring the taste.

He shrugged. "Well, if we resemble each other, and I call you beautiful, does that mean I think I am, too?"

They burst into laughter, and a woman leaving the shop turned and smiled at them.

Patience sighed happily. She liked Jonathan. He was inquisitive and funny, able to laugh at himself and the comments she made.

"You're quick-witted," she told him, her elbows resting on the table.

"And you are adorable and charming. We'd make the perfect pair."

For once, she didn't know how to respond. She wasn't sure if he was joking or not. She didn't want to laugh or make some sarcastic remark, so she just sat there watching him, waiting anxiously for his next move. Honestly, she could have stayed there forever, chatting with him in Brew. There were only a few customers in the place- an elderly couple talking quietly on one of the couches and a middle-aged man reading the paper. A mother stood at the counter while her small child ran around the shop as if s he'd consumed a latte. Patience smiled as she watched the little girl, who couldn't have been more than three years old. Her mom left the counter many times to retrieve the child, holding her hand while trying to dig her credit card out of her wallet.

"Stand still, Sara," the woman hissed through gritted teeth.

"I am, Mommy!" Sara shouted for citizens in neighboring towns to hear. She began hopping up and down on one foot and then the other, her curly red hair flopping into her eyes.

"Mommy, I'm ready to go. I have to go potty. Can I have some of your drink? I'm thirsty! I'm hungry! Do they have candy here? What time is it? Where are the other kids? I want McDonald's. Mommy? Mommy, are you listening?"

Jonathan shook his head. "Sometimes I feel sorry for parents of young children."

She leaned toward him, almost knocking over his latte.

"Surprisingly, she reminds me of my students. Those teens are hyper, fidgety, and loud like her."

He chuckled. "All I can say is I admire you for being a teacher."

* * *

Jonathan walked Patience to her car, his arm draped casually around her shoulders. Although it was almost eleven o'clock, the night was warm and muggy. She couldn't wait for November, when the weather turned slightly cooler. She constantly joked with her parents that she was meant to live in a state that had a nicer climate. But she knew they wouldn't allow her to move. And to be honest, she could not survive living too far away from them.

The two stood in front of her car, about an inch away from each other. She could feel his breath on her cheek as she gazed up at him. He held her hands in his, and she silently thanked God that her palms weren't sweaty.

"I had a great time tonight," he said softly.

"I did, too," she whispered, her heart beginning to pound violently in her chest. Sitting in Brew with him, she'd felt comfortable. But now ...

She waited for him to say something, anything, and wondered if he would try to kiss her.

"I don't want to let you go," he confessed, never letting go of her hands. If he leaned in any closer, their lips would be touching.

"I don't want you to let me go."

"I need to."

She sighed. "No, you don't. We can stand out here all night if you want."

He smiled, letting go of her hands and taking a step backward.

"It's only our first date. And as much as I want to kiss you, I won't. I respect you. Besides, I plan on being around a long time. I want us to take our time and really get to know one another. So I'm going to get in my car and leave."

Patience fought the feeling of disappointment that threatened to surface. If he had tried to kiss her, she would not have resisted. Sure, they were practically strangers, but the time they'd spent together had been like hanging out with an old friend. Plus, it had been ages since she'd kissed a guy. She fought the urge to run after him. She needed to play it cool so she wouldn't scare him off. Yet as she watched Jonathan get into his car, she couldn't help but wonder if he would call.

Chapter 6

Patience slowly made her way down the hall the next morning, her eyes half closed and her pajamas twisted from a rough night's sleep. She'd tossed and turned the majority of the time, thoughts of Jonathan refusing to leave her mind. She wondered who could be knocking at seven a.m. on a Sunday morning. Rory barked uncontrollably, jumping up and down much like the little girl at Brew the night before.

"Cole!"

"Hey, stranger!" Her best friend stepped inside, immediately engulfing her into a huge bear hug. He kissed her cheek tenderly, his arms so tight around her she had to catch her breath. The two held each other as Rory began licking Cole's sneakers, his tail wagging furiously. She could smell his aftershave, and she inhaled deeply, savoring the delicious scent. He pulled away slightly, just far enough so he could look into her eyes.

"I've missed you." His voice broke.

"I've missed you, too." She felt a small lump in her throat, as well.

His dark brown eyes searched her face. "Where have you been?"

Her arms were still around his waist.

"Where have *I* been? You're the one who disappeared."

Two years before, Patience and Cole had taught at the same high school. His degree was in American History, and he also coached football. He loved it. Like her, he adored kids of all ages, and the feeling was reciprocated. The teens idolized him, always coming to him for advice or nominating him for some award such as Teacher of the Year. And with his dark, Cuban good looks and friendly disposition, some of his female students would develop crushes on him, bringing him flowers and home-made goodies. Patience thought it was cute.

Being employed at the same school as her best friend had worked out great for them both. Their classrooms were on different halls, so they didn't get sick of seeing each other. Yet whenever she needed a Cole fix, they could have lunch together or just pop in to say hi. The weird thing was, the two lived only a few miles apart, but sometimes their schedules kept them too busy to go out.

She had been heartbroken when he had transferred to a different school. They had offered him more money and needed him to whip their football team into shape. He was considered one of the best coaches in Dallas, highly respected and knowledgeable in his field. He'd been excited, always up for a challenge. Yet he was also sad to leave Stonebrook High.

The sound of her cell phone drifted into the foyer. She grabbed her handsome friend's arm and practically dragged him into the living room.

"Don't move. I'll be right back," she commanded. Her stomach did a little flip-flop as she sprinted down the hall to her bedroom. She hoped it was Jonathan, although she doubted he would be awake this early. But one never knew. She was an early bird, even on weekends and holidays. Leaping over her bed, she grabbed her iPhone, glancing down at the number before answering. It was her father.

"Crap."

* * *

"So that's it. Claire dumped me." Cole snapped his fingers. "Just like that."

Patience sat on the lawn chair in her backyard, shaking her head out of compassion for her friend. She watched as he threw the tennis ball for Rory to fetch, the sun shining brightly on them all. Cole had waited patiently for her conversation with her father to end, and then the two had fixed pancakes and eggs, laughing and catching up on old times.

"She didn't trust me, plain and simple," he continued. "She blew my phone up constantly, always asking where I was and who I was with."

"That's terrible. Yeah, a relationship cannot survive without trust. It's the glue that holds couples together."

He stooped to pat Rory. "Who are you, Dr. Phil?"

She rolled her pajama sleeves up to her elbows. It was getting pretty warm out.

"I'm being serious, Coley. I don't understand how anyone can handle that pressure. I know I couldn't."

"Me, neither. Do you know how exhausting it is to defend yourself when you've done nothing wrong? Heck, sometimes she had me wondering if I really was cheating on her!"

He walked toward her, sitting down on the lawn chair next

to hers. Rory was at his heels, panting from the long game of fetch.

"I can understand that. When someone behaves irrationally, accusing you of things you haven't done, her paranoia can rub off on you. Luckily, I haven't dated a guy who didn't trust me."

"You're right, Patience. I can't think of a single ex-boyfriend of yours who was possessive." He looked pensive for a moment.

"It's all about attracting people who are mirror images of us. You have a very open and confident spirit. You're trustworthy; therefore, the men in your life act accordingly."

She smiled. "Thanks for saying that. But what about you? From everything I know about Claire, she sounds nothing like you."

"Hmm ... that's true. I don't know how the whole mirror thing applies to me. But it sure sounded good coming out of my mouth."

They laughed. "Yep, you're so philosophical."

Tilting his head, Cole's eyes traveled from the top of Patience's head to the tips of her toes.

"You're still my dream girl, by the way."

"Where did *that* come from?"

He shrugged. "I'm not sure, to tell you the truth. I guess it's because we're sitting here talking about relationships ..."

She wiped a bead of sweat trickling down her neck. "You're everything I could ask for in a guy, as well, minus the fact that you're my brother! Gross!"

His mouth dropped open. "I'm offended. How in the world are we going to get married when you have an attitude like that?"

She giggled, standing up to stretch. Back in high school, the two had made a pact that if neither married by the age of forty, they would become husband and wife.

She stood over him, offering her hand to help him up. He accepted it with a smile, and they stayed there for a while, basking in the warm, cozy feeling their friendship brought. Cole had been correct. She held many of the characteristics he longed for in a mate. If only they hadn't grown up together. If only they weren't so comfortable being around one another. If only the thought of kissing him didn't feel so unnatural. If only . . .

* * *

That evening, Cole and Patience sat in his truck in front of her house listening to music. He had taken her to a matinee and, on the way back, had stopped for an early dinner at The Fish Shack. She was stuffed and knew she wouldn't eat another bite till breakfast the next morning. She glanced over at him, smiling as he snapped his fingers off beat to Marvin Gaye's "Ain't Nothing like the Real Thing." He loved Motown and had a huge collection of CDs by artists such as Stevie Wonder, Aretha Franklin, and The Jackson Five. For someone who liked music with soul and a good beat, he was a terrible dancer and had absolutely no rhythm. Patience had teased him mercilessly throughout the years.

"You can't dance, either," he would always say. "And you're half black!"

"Yeah, well, my mom can't dance, and she's full black."

The two sat a while longer, watching as the neighborhood children played a game of football in the street. They laughed as one of the boys tackled the other, grabbed the ball from him, and began running, his head turned toward the other children. He didn't see the bicycle lying on the grass in front of him and *boom*! He tripped over it, landing with a thud on the grass. The children ran to him, first to make sure he was okay, and then they continued to play.

Patience felt her cell vibrate in her purse next to her feet. Cole was busy thumbing through his CDs, now happily singing along with Smokey Robinson.

"Hello?"

"Hi, it's Jonathan."

Her face lit up. "Hi Jonathan! How are you?"

Cole immediately turned the volume down, swiveling around slightly in his seat to face her.

"I'm great, now that I hear your voice."

Blushing, she fiddled with her purse strap. She could see Cole out of the corner of her eye. He was sitting as still as a statue.

"You're very sweet. Hey, can I call you in about five minutes? I'm about to head inside my house right now."

"Sure."

She began gathering her things, excitement filling her at the thought of talking to him again. He called! She couldn't get out of the truck fast enough, flinging the door open and practically falling out. She dropped the container of leftovers on the curb, rolling her eyes at her clumsiness. Cole laughed.

"*Who* was *that*?" he asked, leaning across the stick shift to give her a hard time.

Slamming the door, she glared at him through the open window.

"Instead of getting out and helping me, you laugh? What kind of friend are you, anyway?"

"Sorry about that. Who were you talking to?"

"His name is Jonathan. We went out last night."

Cole's eyes narrowed. "You went on a date and didn't tell me?"

"Yes."

"Who *is* this guy?"

She pulled the purse strap higher on her shoulder.

"Can we talk about this later? I'm sort of in a hurry."

"Fine." He turned the ignition, preparing to leave.

Patience suddenly felt guilty. She walked over to his side of the truck, her green eyes full of concern. "I'm sorry for being rude. Thank you so much for the wonderful day. I had a great time catching up. We need to do this again really soon, Coley. And I promise I will call you tonight." She leaned inside to hug him with one arm, holding on to her uneaten entrée with the other hand.

He didn't turn to look at her. "Okay, we'll chat tonight."

Chapter 7

"So you have two best friends?" Jonathan asked, his low voice creating goose bumps on Patience's arms.

"Yes. I've known Cole since childhood, and Jana and I met in high school."

"That's interesting. Most people I know only have one good friend."

She laughed.

"Well, leave it to me to go against the grain!"

"You *are* different. I'll just add that to the list of things I like about you."

"Has anyone ever told you how charming you are?"

"No, because you're the only girl I've ever said these things to."

She giggled, opening the fridge to find a snack. It was eight o'clock Sunday evening, and she was starving. The leftovers didn't look as appealing as they had when she'd boxed them up two hours before. Plus, she craved something sweet. She'd been on the phone with Jonathan ever since she'd left Cole sulking outside. She had no idea what had caused his sudden mood change, but the thought hadn't crossed her mind again until now. She wondered if she should let Jonathan go and call her friend to check on him.

Grabbing the huge bowl of banana pudding her mother had made for her, she decided to do the right thing. After all, her best friend came first.

"That's sweet. Listen, I'm going to have to let you . . . "

"Don't let me go," he whined, cutting her off.

She took a huge bite of the dessert, her eyes widening in surprise. They had been on the phone a long time. She couldn't believe he wasn't tired of talking to her yet. However, if he was anything like her, their conversations left Patience wanting more contact, not less. The traits she seemed to be drawn to in men were a sense of humor, being down-to-earth, and a caring nature. If they happened to love animals and children, that was a huge bonus. And he had all of those qualities.

She sighed happily. "Well, I guess I can stay on for a few more minutes."

* * *

At eleven o'clock, Patience and Jonathan finally hung up. She crawled into bed, fully clothed, promising herself she would shower in the morning. Rory was already asleep by her window, tired after chasing squirrels in the backyard, eating a page of one of her student's homework assignments she'd been grading, and digging up some of the flowers in her garden. She wished she had the nerve to spank him sometimes, but she didn't believe in it. And putting a dog in timeout was unheard of, as was grounding or yelling at him. He needed to attend a place like doggie boot camp or something. She didn't know what to do with him.

She laughed to herself, pulling the covers up to her chin, her eyelids feeling heavy. She could picture Jonathan's face perfectly, as if he were lying right beside her. She wondered what it would be like to kiss him. His lips looked soft and inviting, and she could just imagine them on hers, his arms wrapped around her tightly. He was so sexy, the way he moved, the way he talked, the way his eyes burned into hers with intensity and longing . . .

She jumped at the sound of her cell phone.

"Patience," Cole said softly after she'd answered.

Cole!

She sat up in bed, her wild hair falling all around her face and shoulders.

"Oh my gosh! I am so sorry! I was going to call you . . ." She felt horrible.

He sighed. "It's okay."

"No, it is definitely not okay. I swore we would talk tonight, and I dropped the ball. I apologize."

"Patience, would you calm down? Everything is cool. I just wanted to tell you goodnight."

"Aww, you are the sweetest guy ever. Now I feel even worse. But thank you so much." Then she had a thought.

"Hey, I'm taking you out next weekend. You get to pick the night, place and time. It will be my treat."

He laughed. "You have money?"

"Oh, I forgot. I'm always broke. How about if we go dutch?"

"You're on!"

They chatted a bit longer, and then he yawned.

"I hate to let you go but I'm exhausted. Busy day. But we'll talk this week and confirm our plans, sweet lady. How does that sound?"

She smiled. "I can't wait."

"Goodnight, Patience."

"'Night."

* * *

Jonathan held Patience's hand as they strolled through the Dallas Zoo, stopping every couple of seconds so she could coo at one of the animals. He had called her Monday evening, telling her that he'd forgotten to ask her out for a second date. She'd been on cloud nine the entire week, floating through the halls of the high school and totally ignoring the teens who weren't doing what they were supposed to be doing. One of her best students, Talia, hadn't turned in her homework two days in a row, another kept talking during her lecture on American literature, and a third excused himself to go to the restroom and didn't return for twenty minutes. Yet through it all, Jonathan had occupied her mind. The only drawback was that the days seemed to creep by, and she wondered if Saturday would ever get here.

"The monkeys are hilarious," she said in between bites of popcorn.

"Yep, they're pretty cute. I love how that one over there has isolated himself from the rest of the group. He must be an introvert."

She nodded.

"Mmhmm, I totally get that. I mean, do you see how hyper the others are? I'd remove myself, too."

"Did you know some monkeys live on the ground while others live in trees?"

She raised an eyebrow. "Oh? And what other facts do you have about them?"

He took a handful of her popcorn, appearing thoughtful for a moment.

"Depending on what species they are, some eat insects, flowers, or reptiles."

"Blechh! I think I'd want to hang out with the flower-eaters."

The two had a great afternoon getting to know each other even more, enjoying the fun, casual atmosphere of the zoo and the slightly cooler weather. The temperature was ninety-three degrees, so for them, it was like a cold front. They both wore shorts, and Patience had on a tank and sandals, her hair in a ponytail. She looked sixteen, and he could have passed for eighteen. His curly hair was perfect and didn't move despite the wind. It reminded her of Justin Timberlake's hair when he was very young and a part of 'N Sync.

"So, where are we going for our third date?" Jonathan asked as he held his car door open for her. They'd been at the zoo for almost four hours, and she couldn't believe how fast the time had flown by.

"Oh, we're hanging out again?" she asked teasingly.

He started the car. Glancing over at her, he grinned. "Of course."

She folded her arms across her chest.

"My, my, aren't we confident and secure? What if I told you I had a good time but I don't think we're a match?"

"I'd be hurt, disappointed, and sad. And I would decide to

do whatever it took to win you over, because I'm already head over heels for you."

She felt her mouth drop open. She wasn't sure if he was kidding, but he actually sounded serious. She looked out the passenger window, watching the other cars as they drove down the highway. She didn't know what to say, how to respond. All she knew was that she felt the same way he did, if he wasn't joking. She would be sad if he didn't ask her out again. She wanted to be with him as often as she could, and more. She liked the way he made her feel, all warm and giddy with butterflies in her tummy.

"You sure are quiet. Is everything all right?" he asked in the silence. The radio was on but very low, and she had been waiting for him to say something first.

"Everything is wonderful."

"Whew! You had me worried for a sec."

He made small talk as he pulled up to her house, almost hitting her mailbox and running up on her curb. Jonathan seemed not to notice, and Patience hid a smile. She wanted to laugh at the tiny things she noticed about him. He could have hit her car for all she cared. In her eyes, he was near perfect, smart and witty and handsome and a bit crazy. One of the things she liked about him was his honesty. There was no guessing about what he was thinking or where she stood with him. She admired that quality and wished she could be more like that.

"Today was one of the best days of my life," he said softly, his body turned toward her in the seat.

"Oh, come on," she answered, her voice light.

"You don't believe me."

"Forgive me, but it's hard to tell when you're being sarcastic or joking." She wiped her moist hands on her shorts.

He reached out to her, gently holding on to her arm and pulling her to him, until his face was only an inch away from hers.

"Everything I've said to you today has been the truth. I'm crazy about you," he whispered.

Patience held her breath as his lips met hers in a sweet kiss. It was everything she had imagined: soft, tender, and loving. As they parted, she opened her eyes and sighed. What a perfect way to end their date. And she was comfortable enough with him by now to fully enjoy the kiss. If he'd asked her, at that moment, to rob a bank, she would have. Like him, she was head over heels.

"Wow," he exclaimed as he pulled back to look into her eyes. "I knew our first kiss would be amazing, but . . . wow!"

She reached up to run a hand through his curls. "I agree. I figured it would be perfect, and it was." Smiling shyly, she added, "I'm glad you enjoyed it."

His hand still held hers tightly, and they sat quietly for a minute, each lost in thought. With his free hand, he twirled one of her curls around his finger, and then he leaned in for another kiss. His lips lingered on hers, and they could hear a cat meowing in the distance. The sound of a car passing by came next. She was lucky enough to live on a street that didn't get too busy.

"Mmm," she murmured as he ran a finger lightly up and down her arm.

"Patience," he whispered, his breath warm against her cheek.

By the time they exited his vehicle, she was smitten. There was something about him, something she couldn't put into words, that drew her to him. Sure, he had all these great characteristics, and yes, he was so handsome. However, she knew there was more to it than that. She felt magnetically drawn to him. Sitting in his car with him, she hadn't planned on inviting him in. But the words had slipped out before she knew it. And again, it surprised her that he had said yes. They'd spent an entire Saturday together, and like her, he wanted more.

Rory greeted them with enthusiasm and excitement, jumping up on Jonathan wildly.

"Rory, get down," she commanded, reaching over to grab his collar. Jonathan laughed, bending low to pat him. Whenever she had someone new over, it always worried her that her dog would run him or her off. Luckily, only one guest had been scared of him, and by the end of the visit, Rory had won her over.

"He's adorable!" Jonathan exclaimed, a huge grin on his face. When he had picked her up for the zoo, she'd run out before he could meet her crazy pet, but now there was no preventing it. She only hoped Rory wouldn't choke on something like he had when Roman was over, or bug the poor guy to death. Sometimes that could be embarrassing.

"Thanks. He's a pretty good dog." She was delighted he liked animals, which was yet another reason to fall for him.

* * *

It was ten o'clock when Patience walked Jonathan to the door. They had watched an *I Love Lucy* marathon, talking and laughing during commercial breaks. Her sides hurt from stories he'd told her about his childhood, always getting into trouble and pulling pranks on his parents and teachers. He was hilarious, and she hated to see him go. It was ridiculous, really, how the two had spent almost ten hours together, yet she wanted to cry as she stood facing him on the porch.

He took a step closer to her. "Well, I guess this is it."

Shrugging her shoulders, she tried to sound nonchalant. "Yep, I think you're right."

His arms went around her waist, slowly pulling her body as close to his as he could.

"When will I see you again?"

Her green eyes sparkled. "Whenever you want, that's when."

"Tomorrow?"

She tried to think of what she had planned the next day. For some reason, she felt like there was something on her to-do list. She had church in the morning, but there was something else that needed to be done. She furrowed her brows, wondering what on earth it could be.

"Can I let you know tomorrow afternoon? I have to check my calendar."

He threw his head back and laughed.

"Okay, you do that."

"I'm sorry. I would love nothing more than to see you. I don't even want you to leave tonight. Yet I have this nagging suspicion I'm forgetting something, like I have plans but can't remember what they are."

He nodded. "I gotcha. I shouldn't be asking to see you again so soon, anyway. Desperation is not attractive, I suppose."

"It is."

He chuckled. "You're so cute! I will be anxiously awaiting your call. Believe that."

They hugged for an eternity, it seemed. It was the perfect ending to a wonderful day. She watched him walk toward his car, turning once more to blow her a kiss. She thought she would melt right there on her porch, unable to wipe the silly grin off her face. She couldn't wait to run inside and see what she had planned for the next day. Hopefully her time was free and she could spend it with her new crush.

Chapter 8

"I really am sorry."

Cole exhaled slowly, his brown eyes appearing even darker when angry. "It's all right."

Patience hung her head, temporarily unable to look at her friend. She sat on the bar stool next to his in the noisy living room, his two guy friends playing video games a few feet away from them. The night before, as soon as she'd climbed into bed after checking her schedule, it had hit her. She'd totally forgotten her plans with him. She was supposed to have met him at Chili's for appetizers, and then he was going to take her to The Music Hall at Fair Park to see The Lion King. Although neither of them liked sitting through plays or musicals, both had been excited about this particular one. Patience owned the DVD, and Cole always got choked up when Mufasa died.

As soon as she'd realized her mistake, she had called him several times throughout the night and early morning, but to no avail. He wasn't answering. She'd texted and emailed him, also, yet deep down, she knew she'd messed up big-time. Patience had tossed and turned the remainder of the morning, vowing to hightail it over to his house as soon as she let Rory out. Plus, her friend always slept in on weekends like normal people did, so she had to wait until noon to head over there. When she'd pulled up to his house, she'd noticed his friends' cars parked in the driveway, and her heart had sunk. She was disappointed that he had company. She needed privacy to apologize.

Unfortunately, Cole wasn't letting her off the hook easily. When he'd answered the door, his mouth was set in a thin line, and his eyes had narrowed as he looked at her with contempt. She'd swallowed the lump in her throat, following him inside and greeting Jarrod and Cary halfheartedly. Cole had fixed himself a drink and plopped down heavily on the barstool, asking if she wanted something.

"No, thanks. I can't believe you're drinking this early," she observed. He rarely drank, having only a beer or two when they went to a party or get-together.

"Do you care?" he'd asked with a smirk, downing the rum and coke in one gulp.

"Of course I care! You're my friend, and I am so sorry for dissing you last night."

"Whatever."

"I *am* sorry. Please forgive me. I got, um, distracted." She could feel her face get warm, so she lowered her eyes.

Cole sat up straighter. "What distracted you? Or should I ask *who*?"

Silence.

He stood up quickly, sliding the empty glass across the bar in frustration. "Never mind. I already know."

Cary glanced over at them, one eyebrow raised out of curiosity.

Patience pushed the lock of hair off her forehead, her eyes misty with unshed tears.

"Coley, please understand. I didn't purposely ignore you. I forgot, and I feel horrible."

"You should."

She nodded. "Okay, I deserve that. I would be mad, too. But how about I make it up to you? What are you doing tonight?" She tried unsuccessfully to smile.

Walking toward his kitchen, he answered, "I'm busy."

Cary stood then, approaching her with open arms. "Don't beat yourself up too much, Patience. Cole's being an ass. I'm not sure why he's acting like you killed someone, but don't worry about it."

She shook her head. "Nah, he's right. I've been a terrible friend to him lately."

She accepted Cary's hug gratefully, thankful to have at least one ally. She looked up when Cole came back into the room, his shoulders sagging slightly. She couldn't help but notice how handsome her friend was that day, even though he was upset with her. His dark hair was a little longer, almost to his shoulders, and his olive skin appeared flawless. He obviously had been working out, too, for the muscles in his arms were more defined, and his stomach was flat. He'd always had an awesome body, but he was even more toned lately.

He sat down next to Jarrod on the couch as if she weren't there, so she didn't know what to do. Since the whole thing was her fault, she decided to make one last effort to patch things up. She stood next to the guys awkwardly, looking down at her best friend with remorse. She didn't blink as she searched for the right words to say. He didn't look up.

"Would you like to catch a movie tomorrow night?"

He shrugged, his focus on the video games in front of him. "No, thanks. I have plans."

"How about Wednesday? We could take Rory to the park for a nice run."

"I can't Wednesday."

She could feel the lump returning to her throat. "Let's see. Next Saturday Jana's having a party. It would be cool to go together."

Finally he glanced up at her. "I'm going to be sick next Saturday."

That was it. Patience had had it.

She stormed off and began searching for her keys, anxious to get out of there. The air was too thick with hostility and bitterness, and if she stayed one more second, she would end up punching Cole in the throat. He had some nerve, making her grovel and beg for forgiveness this way. She'd made a mistake, forgetting about their plans. Yet she had been a great friend to him over the years. There must have been something else bothering him. Maybe work had him stressed, but she wasn't going to hang around and find out, not with him treating her this way.

Finding her keys on the bar stool she'd been sitting on, she mumbled good bye to Cary and Jarrod, her eyes focused on the front door as she walked quickly toward it. She could hear Cary saying something to the guys as she reached for the doorknob. She was temporarily blinded by the sun shining brightly outside, so she tripped over the newspaper, stumbling forward and into the prickly bushes that lined his porch. She winced from pain, the stinging sensation overtaking her bare arms and legs. It felt as if she'd landed on a beehive.

"Ouch!" Suddenly she felt two strong hands grab her waist, pulling her to safety. She turned around, and it was Cary. He was laughing hysterically.

"Are you okay?" he asked once he'd caught his breath.

"You mean besides the burning of my skin? Sure, I'm great."

"Did you not see the bushes?"

Patience began walking to her car, unable to see humor in the situation.

"I've got to go," she said in a soft voice. All she wanted to do now was lie in a nice bubble bath and unwind.

Cary stood by her car window, sympathy evident in his eyes.

"I'm sorry you're having a bad day. Cole is being unbelievably rude and obnoxious. When you were leaving, I told him to go after you, but he refused. I plan on giving him hell the rest of the day on your behalf."

She laughed as she started the car. "Thanks, Cary. I appreciate that."

He reached over to ruffle her curls. "Anytime. You've always been like a little sister to me."

* * *

Patience entered the quiet house later that evening, her mood lighter than before. After leaving Cole's, she'd headed straight for her parents' house, in desperate need of TLC. Her mother had been thrilled at the surprise visit. John had gone hunting for the weekend, and Sharise told her it was the perfect day to sit around and chill. The two wound up ordering a pizza and watching movies, and then they just sat around talking, enjoying each other's company. She told her mother about Cole and how bad he'd made her feel.

"No one can make you feel anything. That's your job," Sharise said.

"But, Mom, he was so mean! He wouldn't even look at me half the time, and the other half he spat rude words out like darts. I apologized a million times. Geez!"

Sharise tossed some ideas around then, wondering if he always felt neglected whenever Patience met a new guy or if he had a crush on her.

Patience waved a hand dismissively. "That's ridiculous. Coley's like family. We could never feel that way toward each other."

"I'm just sayin' . . . "

The subject was dropped, but as Patience went to let Rory out, she thought about what her mom had said. She just could not imagine him feeling ignored *or* wanting to date her. She shrugged her shoulders, deciding then and there to erase him from her mind. The way he had treated her this morning, she was sure it would be a while before they talked again, anyway.

Chapter 9

By the middle of October, Patience and Jonathan were dating exclusively. They hung out most weeknights together, and on weekends the two usually went out dancing or to a movie or concert. The best thing about their relationship was that it didn't matter what they did, as long as they were together. He had gone to church with her a couple of times, as well, and loved it. He'd invited her to his parents' home for dinner the week before, and they loved her. Cliff and Patricia Brown were friendly and welcoming, going on and on about how Jonathan couldn't stop talking about her. She also instantly clicked with his sister, Lily. Patience was impressed by how smart and mature she seemed to be. Jonathan was right. His parents had done a great job raising her.

The one thing that surprised her was the fact that his parents were African-American. By the looks of him, she'd thought he was biracial when they'd first met. He laughed when she told him later that night.

"I get that a lot," he said. "Most people assume I'm mixed. It's because I have green eyes, light skin, and curly hair."

"I know. As I've said before, you look like me."

"My great-grandfather had green eyes, and my dad's sister

has what we call good hair," he explained. "It's so weird when you think about which genes are dominant or recessive."

She nodded.

"I agree. One would think I'd have brown eyes and a darker skin tone."

"I can't wait to meet your parents," he whispered, kissing her lightly on the lips. "I'm going to thank them for creating you."

And he did. Patience thought he was joking, but he said the same corny thing to John and Sharise. They thought highly of him, too. They'd encouraged her to bring him to their neighborhood's block party, and he had a great time. Her mother was impressed by his manners and the way he hung on to her daughter's every word. John liked his intelligence and enjoyed talking politics and current events with him. She was thrilled they liked him, because she knew deep down he would be around a long time.

On Halloween night, she rushed to get dressed for the party Jonathan's best friend was throwing. Jonathan had asked her to go with him the day before, which was the last minute, in her eyes. They'd brainstormed and decided to dress up as Tarzan and Jane, so her costume was pretty skimpy. It had slightly more material than a bikini, so she was thankful her body could handle a little exposure. She usually chose costumes that were more modest, but as she admired herself in the full-length mirror, she had to admit she looked good. The leopard-print skirt was high on one side and came to her lower thigh on the other.

His eyes almost popped out of his head when he saw her, yet his costume leaned toward the daring side itself. The leopard-print tunic covered only half his chest and tied over one shoulder. It fell slightly above his knees, and she laughed at the matching leopard sash he wore as a headband. To top it off, he carried a fake spear.

"My, my," she began, giving him the once-over admiringly. "Are we going to a party ... or the jungle?"

He pulled her to him, lust evident in his eyes. "We can go wherever you want," he whispered seductively. "And that includes your bedroom."

Patience giggled as he nuzzled her neck, wrapping her arms around his waist tightly. She knew he was all talk. During the past two months of dating him, Jonathan had never tried to sleep with her, which was admirable but, at the same time, mind-boggling. She didn't know whether to be relieved because he obviously liked her for more than her body or disappointed because he could restrain himself so effortlessly. There were days when he would drop her off after their dates when she thought she'd go insane from pent-up desire for him. Making out with him just didn't quite seem to satisfy her as of late, yet she didn't want to pressure him. She was determined to move at the pace he set.

"I missed you today," she cooed instead.

"Me, too," he whispered. Taking a step backward, he released her and shook his head.

"We better leave now or I'll change my mind. I want you all to myself. Plus, I'm not too sure I like the idea of everyone staring at you at Matt's party. Now that I think about it, I don't know if you need to meet my friends. They're all going to hit on you."

"You're crazy!"

"I'm serious."

* * *

Twenty minutes later, Patience was shaking Matt's hand.

"It's nice to meet you," she yelled over the loud music.

They stood in Matt's spacious kitchen, along with about fifteen other people. Apparently, Jonathan's friend was popular, as there appeared to be five hundred guests in his small apartment. And everyone had worn a costume. She was impressed by the creative ideas people came up with. Someone was a Sun-Maid Raisins box, which made her laugh. She wondered how he could see where he was going, not to mention how hot it probably was in there. She saw Beauty and the Beast, Mr. and Mrs. Potato Head, a bunch of pirates, and tons of mermaids. She couldn't stop laughing at two girls dressed as bacon and eggs. She pointed them out to Jonathan, who just rolled his eyes with a smile.

When they'd arrived at the party, the door had been open, and Jonathan had immediately gone into protective mode, grabbing her hand while walking in front of her. They'd had to weave through the wild, energetic crowd in search of Matt, eventually finding him in the kitchen mixing drinks. She guessed he was supposed to be Robin Hood but wasn't sure.

His friend was nothing like what she had imagined. When Jonathan described him, she'd pictured someone who had the same characteristics as him: tall and thin, with medium brown skin and glasses. However, Matt was shorter than her, probably five foot five, with a very muscular build and dark complexion. He was attractive but reeked of arrogance, almost as if he knew he was handsome. He didn't appear studious like Jonathan, either. Had she seen him on the street, she would've thought he was an athlete or bodyguard.

"You, too," he replied, his smile fading slightly as he studied her. He let go of her hand, his dark eyes traveling over her body and finally resting on her face. She felt as if he were sizing her up, almost the way a parent would his daughter's new boyfriend.

Jonathan grabbed Matt, patting him on the back affectionately. "I'm so glad you two finally get to meet! I've told her a lot about you, man."

Matt raised an eyebrow. "Yeah?"

"Yep, I sure did. She knows everything, how you're like a brother to me."

"That's cool." His friend shrugged, returning to the counter to continue making the drinks. Someone on a skateboard suddenly came through the kitchen, almost knocking Patience off balance. Jonathan caught her, yelling after the guy to watch where he was going. She laughed, not used to hearing him curse or look angry.

"Some people are idiots!" he hissed, putting his arm around her shoulders to pull her close. "You're not leaving my side tonight. If you have to go to the restroom, I'm going with you."

She kissed his cheek. "Honey! That's really sweet, but I can take care of myself."

"Nuh uh. I have a bad feeling about tonight already." As soon as the words came out of his mouth, they heard a scream. Matt ran out of the kitchen, followed by Jonathan and Patience. Three guys were fighting in the bedroom, and a girl who was trying to break it up was pushed by one of them. As Matt jumped in, Jonathan grabbed Patience by the waist, preventing

85

her from getting involved as well. She was known for butting in when someone was getting hurt or needed rescuing, although it was usually none of her business. Once, she'd stopped a mother from spanking her child in a restaurant. Cole had been with her, and he'd sat at their table, acting as if he didn't know her. The dining area was packed, but no one had said anything as the woman began yelling at the disobedient child, threatening to knock some sense into him. What shocked Patience the most was the age of the boy. He appeared to be in middle school.

Jonathan ordered her to stay put, and then he went to help Matt, who was already bleeding from his mouth. The fight escalated, and two other guys joined in. It was crazy. She prayed that Jonathan wouldn't get hurt, and she fought the urge to wedge herself in the middle, knowing deep down it wouldn't solve anything. Besides, she wasn't in the mood to get punched or knocked down, and he would be ticked if she put herself in danger.

Finally, after what seemed an eternity, two husky body-builder types literally picked up the man who'd started the whole mess, carrying him outside and to his car. Patience doubted he was in good enough condition to drive, and she was relieved to hear his girlfriend say she could drive him home. Amazingly, the party was still going on in most areas of the apartment. Only the guests in the front room had paused to witness the fight. Many of the onlookers were either drunk or too self-involved to notice.

She ran to the kitchen, returning seconds later with a wet cloth and ice pack for Matt. She found him in the restroom, leaning forward over the sink to closely inspect his cuts and bruises. Their friend Vic stood in the doorway, worry etched on his face as he told Matt he was losing way too much blood.

"I already have one mama," Matt informed him irritably. "I don't need two."

"Here you go," she interrupted, handing Vic the towel and ice pack to give to Matt.

"Thanks!" Vic accepted the items gratefully and passed them to his friend.

Matt didn't respond, turning the faucet on to wash his face.

"Here, Patience was nice enough to bring you these."

"I don't need them."

"It appears as if you do," Vic said, thrusting the towel in his hand.

Matt ignored him, his face dripping wet as he turned off the light and squeezed between Vic and the doorframe, bumping into her roughly as he returned to the party.

Vic turned to her.

"What an ass!"

She stood with her arms folded across her chest, unsure of what to say. She wanted to agree but kept her mouth closed. Out of all the friends she'd met that night, Vic was the sweetest. He hovered over her now, his tall, lanky body giving her the impression he was either a basketball player or model. He was gorgeous, with medium-length blond hair pulled back into a ponytail and blue eyes the color of the sea. He wore a convict costume and had a ball and chain wrapped around his ankle.

"It's okay," she replied with a smile. "I'd be irritable, too, if my face was gushing blood."

He shook his head. "You're too forgiving. He's been rude to you all evening."

"Maybe he didn't like the movie *Tarzan*," she joked, trying to lighten the mood.

Vic frowned, casually throwing his arm around her shoulders as they headed toward the living room.

"Well, then, he needs to be rude to Jonathan, not you!"

The two laughed, weaving through the crowd carefully.

"Can I get you something to drink?" he shouted over the music.

"That's okay. If she's thirsty, *I* will get it for her," Jonathan cut in, approaching the two and reaching over to lift Vic's arm off her shoulders.

"That's cool," his friend said with a smile. "I was just taking care of her while you were busy."

"Thanks, man," Jonathan replied sarcastically. "I appreciate that."

Vic wandered off, and a few minutes later, they saw him dancing with a girl dressed as a witch.

"Dang! I *knew* I shouldn't have brought you here! Everyone's falling in love with you."

Patience laughed.

"Everyone except Matt ..." she mumbled under her breath.

* * *

"Whew! What a night!" Jonathan exclaimed as he sat on the couch next to Patience three hours later. The two were still at Matt's, and there were about ten others lagging behind. A couple was making out heavily in the dining room, five guys were playing cards out on the balcony, and some were dancing or chatting amongst themselves. It had been an eventful night.

Not long after the fight, she had watched a guy break up with his girlfriend, and two people had gotten sick right in front of her. Also, someone had tripped over the steps leading to Matt's bathroom, bumping his head on the wall in front of him. He wound up being okay, but there was a huge knot on his forehead and tears in his eyes.

She nodded her head in agreement, turning to address Matt, who was sitting in the La-Z-Boy chair across from them. She smiled.

"Yes it was! Wow, you sure do throw interesting parties."

He looked at her, saying nothing. He took a sip of his beer, his expression blank.

Jonathan chuckled. "Sweetie, you should have seen your face when that girl threw up all over the kitchen floor. I'm surprised *you* didn't get sick."

Swatting playfully at him, she laughed.

"Thanks a lot. I can't help it if some things gross me out!" Turning back to Matt, she said,

"Did you have to clean it up? Hopefully your best friend volunteered to do it for you!"

Matt shrugged as he took another sip of his drink. His focus was on the wall behind her.

Jonathan defended himself. "If he had asked, I would have."

Matt laughed sarcastically, leaning back with his eyes closed. "Yeah, right. We all know you have a sensitive stomach. You're just playing tough right now."

Patience listened as the two began visiting memory lane, recounting stories about the time Jonathan had gotten sick after riding The Texas Giant at Six Flags. That led to a whole conversation on throwing up, getting carsick, and hangovers. She tried jumping in with a few comments here and there, but to no avail. Anything she said, Matt ignored. And Jonathan seemed oblivious to the fact that his friend didn't seem to like her. After a while, she decided to get some fresh air. Not bothering to excuse herself, she stood and headed toward the balcony.

"Where ya going, sweetie?" Jonathan called after her.

"Outside," she responded, her back to him as she joined the guys who were playing cards.

"Hold on, I'll join you!"

"Wow, she's hot," she overheard one of Matt's friends say as she passed the table. Leaning against the rail, she inhaled deeply, coughing as secondhand smoke filled her lungs. Three out of the five card players were smoking.

So much for the fresh air, she thought to herself.

"Sweetheart! Why did you leave me?" Jonathan was next to her in no time, a worried look in his eyes.

"I just needed a change of scenery, is all."

"What's wrong?"

She shrugged. "Nothing is wrong."

Putting his arms around her, he pulled her close. "Yes, something's bothering you. Tell me."

Patience sighed. "I get the feeling Matt isn't too fond of me."

"What makes you say that?"

"He doesn't make eye contact, usually staring at my forehead or the wall behind me. He ignores most of what I say, and when he does respond, it's just a nod here or an *mmhmm* there. I get the impression I'm rubbing him the wrong way."

A couple of their friends who were playing cards fell silent, their heads turned toward her.

"He can be standoffish when he first meets someone,"

Jonathan reassured, his voice softening a bit at the sight of their audience.

"Really?" she asked, tilting her head to the side as she gazed up at him.

"Yes, I promise that's what it is. Once he gets to know you better, I'll have to beat him off of you with a stick. You'll see."

He kissed her, his arms still wrapped tightly around her waist. "Tell you what. How about we plan a date with Matt and his girlfriend for next weekend?"

"He has a girlfriend?" The words slipped out before she could stop them. She instantly felt her cheeks flush from embarrassment. She didn't want to give the impression she wasn't crazy about his friend. The card players laughed, and Jonathan couldn't hide his amusement.

"Yep, believe it or not, he does!"

Chapter 10

"So, what did y'all think of the movie?" Patience asked, her heart still racing as they left the theater. She couldn't stand horror flicks and knew she would not sleep for the next week, but she tried to shrug it off as best as she could. She didn't want everyone to know how much of a scaredy-cat she was. Jonathan squeezed her hand affectionately in the backseat of Matt's BMW, his gaze sympathetic.

"I hated it," Matt's girlfriend, Tricia, stated.

"I didn't like it because my baby was scared to death," Jonathan cooed, a half smile tugging his lips.

Patience shuddered.

"Why in the world would someone willingly run into the woods at night? I mean, the guy was chasing her with a chain-saw! She should've headed down the street where the other houses were. Maybe someone could've helped her."

Tricia nodded from the front seat. "And I knew she would trip and fall. But why did she start crawling instead of jumping back up on her feet and running? That was stupid. Of course he caught up with her!"

Jonathan chuckled. "I'm glad he killed her. All that screaming got on my nerves."

Matt stopped the vehicle at a red light, his eyes straight ahead as the others chatted about the movie. When the light turned green, the truck in front of them didn't go immediately, so he honked.

"Sweetheart, I can't stand when you honk at other drivers. That is so rude."

"Green means go, and they just sat there!"

Tricia pretended to tighten her seat belt. Matt adjusted his rearview mirror while she continued to complain about his driving.

"It just makes me nervous," she went on. "Haven't you heard of road rage? What if we get shot? And of course the police would blame you, the black man."

Patience snickered, and Matt quickly glanced at her over his shoulder. Jonathan reached over to pat Tricia on the top of her head.

"Don't worry. I'll testify on his behalf."

"You'll be dead from the shooting," she retorted grumpily.

"Quit being so dramatic," Matt said as he pulled the car into the restaurant's parking lot. "You always blow things way out of proportion."

Tricia reapplied her lip gloss before responding. She was a cute girl, very short and curvy, with dark skin and full lips. She wore her hair in tight braids that fell just below her shoulders. She had quite a bit of makeup on, and Patience wondered what she looked like underneath it all. Her guess was that she was even prettier without all the face paint on.

"I don't care what you say. Your impatience and recklessness are going to get us into a heap of trouble one day."

Fifteen minutes later, the four were in the restaurant looking over the menu. Patience sat next to Jonathan and across from Matt, which made her nervous. She caught him staring at her a couple of times before the waiter came with their drinks. Yet instead of smiling or looking away, he would study her face and hair, and then his eyes would return to the others. After a while, she decided she was being paranoid, so she attempted to strike up a conversation with him instead.

"Did you grow up in Texas?" she asked pleasantly.

"Yes."

"Do you like it here?"

"Yes."

She glanced at Tricia, who shrugged her shoulders as she listened. Jonathan began tapping the rim of the glass with his spoon.

"So, what did *you* think of the movie?" she asked with a smile, wiping her damp palms on her napkin.

"Loved it," he answered, not bothering to look up from the menu.

Jonathan spoke up. "Are you serious? The movie sucked."

"What did you like about it?" Patience asked Matt, taking a sip of water and not really wanting to know his answer.

"Everything."

She forced another fake smile. "So you're a fan of scary movies, huh?"

"Yep."

She had expected one-word replies to her questions, so she wasn't surprised. But at least Jonathan could see now that she hadn't imagined Matt's lack of enthusiasm toward her.

"I didn't know you liked horror films!" Tricia cut in. "You

told my brother there aren't enough blacks in them, and that the ones who are cast get killed off first."

Jonathan laughed. "That does sound like something he'd say."

The waiter came and took their orders. Matt went first.

"I'll have the fajitas."

"Mmm, that sounds good. I think I'll have that, too," Patience said, brushing a stray curl off her forehead.

His eyes narrowed. "Um, on second thought, let me have the salmon with steamed veggies."

She looked at Jonathan, her mouth hanging open in shock. She wondered how someone could be so blatantly rude all the time. And she was also getting upset because Jonathan was ignoring it. He should say something.

Instead, he winked. "I'll have the fajitas, as well."

"Make that three orders," Tricia said loudly, shooting Matt a dirty look.

* * *

"What is up with him?" she asked Patience later in the ladies' room. The two had excused themselves midway through their entrees to have some girl talk.

"Matt doesn't like me."

Tricia put her hands on her hips. "I can tell. But why?"

"I'm not sure."

"I'll ask him."

As Patience washed her hands, Tricia reapplied her maroon lipstick, suddenly frowning at her reflection.

"Uh oh, I just remembered something Matt told me a while ago," Tricia began.

Patience grabbed a paper towel, a frown forming on her lips as well. "What?"

"Well, when Matt and I first met, Jonathan was dating this girl who works at the mall. She was a real witch, always acting like a princess, wanting people to bow down to her. None of Jonathan's friends liked her, and of course, Matt couldn't stand her. Needless to say, the relationship was brief. We were all glad she was out of the picture. But one night Matt was talking about fixing Jonathan up with a co-worker of his, and I told him he didn't need to play matchmaker. Jonathan can find someone by himself. Matchmaking usually backfires anyway."

"And . . . ?"

"Matt started bragging about how Jonathan won't date someone if Matt doesn't approve of her."

Patience leaned against the sink, her eyes narrowed. "Are you serious?"

"Yes, I am. Those two are like brothers. They grew up together and have a really tight bond. They each swore a long time ago that no girl would ever come between them."

"That's the most ridiculous thing I've ever heard!"

"I know," Tricia agreed. She threw up her hands. "But what can you do?"

Patience turned to face the mirror as the words sank in.

"I wonder what it is about me Matt finds repulsive."

Tricia smiled sympathetically. "I wouldn't say you repulse him. To me, it appears you get on his nerves, or under his skin. It's easy to see." She shrugged. "If it makes you feel any better,

I can tell Jonathan adores you. He absolutely turns to mush when looking at you."

Patience hugged her. "Thank you for being so nice to me tonight. Despite Matt's attitude, I've had fun." She held the door open for her as they exited the restroom.

"Me, too. I have to be honest, though. When I first saw you, I made up my mind that I wasn't going to like you."

Patience raised an eyebrow. "Why?"

"Because you're gorgeous. When Jonathan introduced us, all I could think was how unfair life is sometimes. You're beautiful *and* sweet. At least if you were snobbish, I'd have a good excuse to loathe you."

The girls giggled as they made their way back to the table. The guys were debating which teams would make it to the Super Bowl that year. Catching sight of Patience, Jonathan hopped up quickly to pull her chair out for her.

"Thanks, sweet pea," she cooed. She silently thanked God for blessing her with him. She tried not to take him for granted, knowing that all men were not as great as him. Some of her friends had gorgeous boyfriends with zero personality. Others she knew had to sacrifice good looks in exchange for a sweet or thoughtful man. However, so far, Jonathan appeared to be the whole package.

Taking a huge bite of salmon, Matt rolled his eyes. Tricia sighed dramatically, pulling out her own chair noisily.

"I guess Jonathan is the only gentleman left these days," she said with a look of disgust. "Patience, hold on to him for dear life."

"I will," she assured, her tone light but filled with sincerity.

Jonathan blushed. "Oh, come on. I'm not all that."

"Yes, you are," both girls sang in unison, as the family in the booth next to them glanced their way and smiled.

Matt stared down at his plate, pushing his vegetables around with his fork.

Tricia winked. "I think it's wonderful when a man pulls a chair out or holds the door open for a lady." She turned to him. "Come to think of it, you've never let me order first or walked me to my door, and we've been dating nine months!"

"Is that all?" Matt replied, leaning back in his seat with his arms crossed over his chest.

Tricia's mouth fell open, and Jonathan cleared his throat uncomfortably, while Patience played with her napkin. The restaurant was getting busier, and all the booths and tables were occupied around them. A group of rowdy teenagers laughed loudly across the room. A woman dining alone at the table next to theirs shouted into her cell phone, asking her boyfriend if he could hear her.

The four ate in silence a while, no one knowing what to say next. Matt's lack of people skills brought awkwardness to the evening. Finally Tricia spoke up.

"Why don't you like Patience?"

Jonathan dropped the glass he was holding, which the waiter had just refilled with Coke. The brown soda splashed all over his shirt and the remainder of his fajitas before trickling off the side of the table to the carpet. Patience gasped, her hand flying to her mouth in surprise. She hadn't thought Tricia was going to ask him *tonight*, in front of everyone. Jonathan grabbed a bunch of napkins and began cleaning the spill, yet the flimsy tissues weren't absorbent enough to soak up the entire beverage. The hostess came with some rags, and Matt stared at Tricia in amazement.

"What the ...?" he started, but she held up her hand to shush him.

"Don't try to deny it," she ordered. "A blind man could see how you've been treating her differently than everyone else. What's up?"

Patience held her breath. She sat up straight in her chair, unable to take her eyes off his face. Studying his body language intently, she searched for clues that could solve the case before he actually spoke. Jonathan didn't move beside her, and she was certain he wasn't breathing, as well.

Matt shrugged. "She's all right."

That was it. His response contained only three words. He wore a bored expression, scanning the restaurant for their server, who came a few minutes later with their check. Patience didn't believe him. On the contrary, the more time she spent in his presence, the more convinced she became that he couldn't stand her.

Jonathan picked up the check, reaching into his back pocket for his wallet.

"What do you mean, she's 'all right'?"

Matt pulled a credit card out of his own wallet with a smirk. "You know exactly what I mean."

"No, I don't."

At that moment, a young couple entered the restaurant hand-in-hand. The African-American man and Caucasian woman appeared to be in their early thirties and were well dressed. They stood near the door, waiting to be seated. He let go of her hand to touch her cheek softly, leaning forward to whisper in her ear. She smiled adoringly at him. His arm went around her shoulders then, and soon the hostess approached with a friendly greeting, leading them to their table while making small talk.

"Damn! Jungle fever strikes again. People should stick to their own race," Matt commented, rising from his chair and shaking his head. He handed the waiter his Visa as the others stood quietly looking at him. No one said a word while waiting for the waiter to return. Patience could feel her cheeks burning, certain they were the color of crimson. Tricia clenched her fists at her sides, her lips in a tight line. Jonathan pushed his chair in slowly, avoiding eye contact with anyone except their server, who finally made it back with their receipt. The three followed Matt through the double doors, no one daring to speak.

Chapter 11

The ride home was torturous for Patience. She sat in the back-seat with Jonathan, staring out the window into the darkness. The only sound came from the sports station on the radio, which was on low volume. Matt drove at record speed, as if trying to get Patience home as soon as possible. She was slightly nervous that he knew where she lived now. Knowing him, she would probably come home to a mob of picketers on the sidewalk, holding up signs about biracial people being ze-bras and interracial couples needing to be banned from society. She began twirling a lock of her hair with her finger, the texture somewhat frizzy from the slight humidity of the night air.

As Matt entered her neighborhood, a huge feeling of relief overcame her. She was almost home. In less than two minutes, she would be able to escape the presence of this egotistical, obnoxious, closed-minded knucklehead for good. She couldn't wait to dive into her cozy bed with a good book. It had been a long night, sitting on pins and needles as she waited for this guy to accept her for who she was. She was also disappointed in Jonathan, who hadn't defended her or addressed the issue.

Before the car came to a complete stop, she flung the door open and practically sprinted up the driveway to her safe haven.

She heard Tricia yell out the window that it was great meeting her, so she did turn around quickly once she reached the porch to wave at her. She noticed that Jonathan was close behind her, and even in the darkness, she could see the concern etched on his handsome face. She fumbled around for the keys, the sound of Rory's barking coming from inside.

Jonathan stood behind her as she turned the key in the lock.

"Patience?" he whispered, his warm breath tickling the back of her neck.

"Yeah?" She didn't turn around.

"You can't look at me?"

Slowly she turned to face him, hurt by the way the night had turned out.

He took a step closer to her, and now they were only an inch apart. His green eyes bore into hers.

"I'm so sorry. Matt and I are going to have a long conversation after we drop Tricia off."

She cocked her head to one side, her curly hair falling over one shoulder.

"About what?"

He shrugged. "I'm going to find out why he was such an ass tonight."

She took a step backward. "I can tell you why. He can't stand me because I'm biracial. You don't need to waste your breath asking him why he was so rude."

He shook his head. "I don't know why he made that comment about the interracial couple earlier. He's not like that. Something else must be bothering him."

"What? Are you kidding me? Jonathan, he said just what

he feels. Why are you questioning it? And why didn't you say something back at the restaurant, or in the car, for that matter?"

"I didn't want to cause a scene."

"That's so ridiculous."

The two jumped when Matt honked, signaling for Jonathan to hurry up. Patience nodded toward him.

"Your master is calling."

"What's that supposed to mean?"

"Tricia told me you won't date anyone without his approval."

He threw his head back and laughed. "That's not true."

"Are you sure?"

Leaning in closer, he gave her a quick peck on the cheek. "I'll call you when I get in."

She opened the door, and Rory jumped up on her excitedly.

"All right, I'll talk to you later then."

* * *

"So what did he say?" Patience asked, her head at the foot of her bed so she could snuggle with Rory. She patted his soft fur absentmindedly. He yawned, his eyes closed but his tail wagging from contentment. He relished the extra attention given to him that night. After being rejected by Matt, she thirsted for the unconditional love of her pet. Dogs were very therapeutic in situations such as these, when humans could be so cruel, judgmental, and heartless.

Jonathan sighed heavily into the phone. "I hate to admit it. You were right. When we were alone in the car, Matt let me have it. I won't go into details, but I found out he doesn't believe in race mixing."

She gazed up at the ceiling, glad she already had her pajamas on. Now she wouldn't have to muster up the strength to get undressed after they hung up. Suddenly her limbs felt heavy, and it would've been hard to complete even the simple task of putting clothes on. At least she lived alone, so she could have slept in the nude if wanted to.

"Are you there?" he asked, his voice soft.

"Yes."

"What are you thinking?"

Giving Rory one last pat, she rolled over to the head of the bed. She needed her pillows.

"To be honest, I'm worried. Matt's your buddy. Actually, he is a part of your family, like a brother to you. If he doesn't like me, that's it. We're finished. And I don't think I'm strong enough to handle that right now. I really like you."

"Aww! Baby, I *more* than like you! These past months have been the best in my life. You mean the world to me. Don't even think about Matt. He'll come around."

"And if he doesn't?"

"He will."

Patience sat up in her bed, the covers falling to her waist. "Jonathan! Suppose he still hates me a month from now."

"Baby, will you please stop fretting? Think positive! You're a wonderful person. Anyone would be a fool not to fall for you."

"Fine, I will keep an open mind. Just promise me one thing."

"Yes, ma'am."

"If Matt and I end up enemies, it won't affect my relationship with you. I can't lose you."

"I promise."

* * *

Jonathan's friend Vic threw a party the second weekend in November, and Patience was invited. It thrilled her that most of his friends were nice and fun to be around. Gerald, a buddy he worked with at Chili's, had been the class clown in high school, and she could see why. He was hilarious, always cracking jokes and doing impersonations of professional football players, politicians, and actors. Braxton, a new friend who sat behind Jonathan in one of his classes at UT, was extremely shy, barely muttering hello to her when they'd met at Matt's party. Yet he had a sweet disposition, helping her up when she'd missed a step leading to Matt's hallway. He hadn't laughed like some of the other guests.

Jana helped Patience with her hair and makeup the night of the party. Jonathan was due to pick her up shortly, and Jana was running late, as usual. So their time to give Patience a different look was limited. Usually she didn't care about her appearance, but she woke up that morning with the urge to look older and more sophisticated. Jana didn't understand. Her motto in life was: *If it ain't broke, don't fix it.*

She pulled Patience's hair up with a silver clip, allowing some of her curls to fall loosely by her ears and the nape of her neck. Next, she applied makeup in fall colors, such as brown eye shadow and plum lipstick. The mascara she used made her eyelashes appear inches longer, and the smoky lip liner gave the impression that Patience had full lips. She wore a simple black turtleneck and short skirt with heels. Stepping in front of the full-length mirror with Jana behind her, she gasped.

"Oh my goodness, who is that model standing in front of us? And what has she done with Patience?" The girls burst into a fit of giggles, and Rory left the room. He was not amused by all the makeup talk.

"Jonathan is going to freak when he sees you."

* * *

And he did. His eyes nearly popped out of his head when he picked her up. Yet surprisingly enough, he kept commenting on how beautiful she was without a bunch of face paint on.

"Sweetie, all that does is hide your flawless complexion and gorgeousness. Who talked you into this? Jana, I bet."

Patience laughed as she chose a CD in his car. Vic didn't live far from her, it turned out, so she had no time to be nervous about seeing Matt.

"It was *my* idea, sweet guy. I wanted a different look for tonight. Is that a crime?"

"Yes, it most certainly is. Why mess up a good thing?"

"You sound like Jana now!"

"She's a smart woman," he said playfully, and five minutes later, they were pulling into a neighborhood with houses so big they could've been mansions.

"Vic lives here?" She almost got whiplash twisting her neck to get a good look at the huge home they passed.

"He still lives with his parents, who are out of town this weekend."

"Oh, that explains it. I thought Vic had money, but apparently his mother and father do."

Jonathan chuckled. "Yeah, Vic's broke. He goes to school full time, but I still don't know what his major is. He's a junior at North Texas and changes his major once a semester. To be honest, I think he's afraid to grow up. What a shame. He's a smart guy and is good with kids. I told him he needs to be a teacher or counselor. He didn't take that advice seriously, though."

"Mmm, that is sad. He could also be a model. He's so attractive. Has he considered acting?"

There were so many vehicles on the street that Jonathan had to park at the next-door neighbor's house. Turning the car off, he faced Patience squarely before getting out.

"Vic is attractive, huh?" A smirk tugged at his lips.

She blushed. "He is, sort of … I mean, if you like the ruggedly handsome type."

He took her hand, leaning in to kiss her softly on the lips. When they parted, he sighed.

"This is the last party I'm bringing you to. All my friends think you're hot, and now I learn that you're attracted to one of them. This is not good."

She smiled, reaching up to ruffle his curls. "Believe me, you have nothing to worry about. I'm yours only."

They kissed again, this time more passionately than before. He placed one hand on her neck, his mouth softly nibbling her upper lip as a moan escaped her. Her hand was on his knee, and she slowly began to move it upward to his thigh. His lips were moist and soft, parting even more to invite her tongue inside. She could feel her heart thumping violently in her chest, temporarily forgetting their surroundings. Night had already fallen, and they could hear the music coming from Vic's place.

With her eyes closed, Patience arched her back as she whispered Jonathan's name, unable to stifle the passion burning inside her. She wanted him. More than anything, she wanted him to make love to her right there in his car. She felt his hand begin to travel downward to her chest, so she arched even more, ready and willing to do whatever he asked. He grazed her breast lightly, and then she heard him groan as he pulled his hand away quickly. She tried unsuccessfully to hide her disappointment, sitting back in the seat dramatically.

"I'm sorry," he choked out, unable to look her in the eyes. They watched a truck pull up across the street from them, and five guys exited soon after, anxious to get to Vic's.

"What's wrong, sweetheart?" she asked, needing to know why he never tried to sleep with her. She knew he was attracted to her, but something was holding him back. Lord knows he couldn't have been afraid of rejection. About a month after they'd started dating, she'd practically forced herself on him, so that wasn't it. Now she understood how men felt when their advances were either ignored or turned down.

He looked straight ahead. "Can we talk about this later? We probably need to get going."

She felt her heart sink. "Okay, let's go."

She didn't wait for him to come around and open her door as he usually did. Putting her purse underneath the seat, she flung the door open with such force she thought it would come off the hinges. Immediately, she began power walking toward the house, and she heard him call for her to wait. She held her head high and kept walking, her focus solely on the wild party ahead. She was so embarrassed, thinking about how she'd almost given her body to a guy who obviously didn't reciprocate the lustful feelings.

Reaching the front steps that led to Vic's house, Patience finally paused to catch her breath. Jonathan arrived a millisecond later, his green eyes flashing.

"What is wrong with you?" he asked, sounding irritated.

"What's wrong with me?" she responded incredulously. Placing her hands on her hips, she stood tall, trying to salvage what little pride she had left.

"Jonathan, I'm sorry. Give me a minute to lick my wounds, okay? We obviously have different levels of, um, attraction toward each other."

At that moment the front door burst open, and a group of scantily clad girls came running out. One of them slowed a bit to eye Jonathan seductively, but then her friend pulled her away. Patience squared her shoulders, standing tall.

"C'mon, let's get this over with."

He nodded. "Sure, that sounds good. We won't stay too long. I need to talk to you."

The party was in full swing as she followed Jonathan through the living room. She came to the conclusion that Vic's parents were either famous celebrities or drug dealers. Their house was huge. She couldn't believe that, despite the size, there were wall-to-wall guests. Someone bumped into her hard, pushing her into Jonathan's back. She turned around but couldn't tell who the culprit was.

"Vic!" Jonathan spotted his friend at the top of the stairs with a girl on each arm.

"Hey, Buddy," Vic yelled back. He released the girls and headed down to greet them, a big smile on his face.

"Patience, I'm so glad you could make it," he said sincerely, kissing her cheek tenderly. The three jumped when they heard a scream come from the backyard, but Vic waved a hand dismissively.

"I have no idea who that is. Someone keeps screaming at the top of her lungs every thirty minutes or so. This party has been crazy. I don't know half the people here."

Jonathan laughed. "You're so popular. I'm jealous."

Patience scanned the crowd and her heart sank. Matt emerged from the hallway with Tricia at his side. Both did not seem thrilled to be there.

"Patience!" Tricia's eyes lit up when she caught sight of her, and Patience screamed with glee. The girls hugged tightly.

"I am so happy to see a familiar face!" Tricia shouted. "This night has been interesting, to say the least."

Matt rolled his eyes. "Women," he muttered irritably. "They can be so dramatic."

Ignoring her boyfriend, she grabbed Patience's arm when Michael Jackson's "Smooth Criminal" came on. "Let's go dance! This is my song."

The two managed to find an empty space to dance in the middle of the living room.

"So how are you?" Patience shouted to her new friend.

"I'm good. Matt has gotten on my last nerve, though. I swear I don't know why I stay with him!"

"I'm sorry! You two will work it out. You're a great person. He'd be crazy to let you go." As she yelled the encouraging words, she caught Matt staring at her from across the room. She tried to smile but knew it didn't look sincere. He quickly turned away, his attention back on the conversation he was having with Jonathan.

"I agree!" Tricia screamed as someone bumped into her. "I may be too good for him, to tell the truth." She winked.

Patience laughed. "You most likely are."

They danced to two more songs, occasionally making comments about the other guests or the music. Afterward, the two headed to the kitchen for water. As they stood chatting, Jonathan approached, his expression serious. He gave a quick nod to Tricia and then reached for Patience's hand.

Giving her a kiss on the cheek, he whispered softly, "I missed you."

Tricia excused herself discreetly, leaving them alone for a moment.

Patience smiled, her mood lifting somewhat. "I missed you, too."

Her back was against the counter, and she gazed up at him, their bodies only an inch apart. His arms went around her waist, and she breathed in the delicious scent of his cologne. He pulled her closer, their bodies pressed together now as she wrapped her arms around his neck. With her fingertip, she slowly began to tickle the back of his neck. He grinned.

"That feels good. I love the way you touch me. It sends tingles up my spine."

She giggled. "You have the same effect on me."

He moved in for another kiss but was interrupted by a couple of guests bursting into the kitchen. He took hold of her hand, lust evident in his eyes, and she followed him upstairs. They chose Matt's bedroom, as all the others were taken, and they began making out with a passion so intense neither of them could fight it. She shuddered as his hands explored her body, and she knew there was no turning back. They were so in tune with each other in the darkness, caressing and teasing, her lips nibbling on his earlobe while he whispered her name over and over.

Pressing her body into his, she could feel that he was aroused, which turned her on even more. Her hands made their way to his butt, and she squeezed gently as he moaned. She arched her back, her breasts pressed against his hard chest, his lips devouring hers hungrily.

Patience wanted him so badly she couldn't stand it. She felt his warm hands underneath her blouse, beginning at her waist and moving upward, stopping below her breasts.

"Touch me," she said quietly, almost to the point of panting.

Jonathan hesitated. She couldn't see his face in the dark, so she tried kissing him again, but he pulled back slightly. His hands returned to her hips, and she sighed heavily.

"Turn on the light," she commanded. When he didn't, she searched for the switch herself, feeling her way around the unfamiliar room, but she couldn't find it.

"I want to explain."

But she didn't want to hear it. She was ready to go home.

"Can we please just leave?"

They stood in the middle of the room, and he had a firm grip on her skirt. She had no choice but to stay put.

"I'm going to release you now while I turn the light on. Promise me you won't dart out the door."

To her own surprise, she nodded.

Once they could see each other, he motioned for her to sit

on the bed and she complied. He did the same. Turning to her, he ran a hand through his hair in frustration.

"First of all, I need to apologize for my rudeness earlier. I have been extremely unfair to you. I owe you an explanation."

"Yes, that would be nice."

His eyes clouded. "I'm sorry. It's just . . ."

She placed her hand on his. "What is it? Just tell me."

Chapter 12

"I'm a virgin."

Patience stared at Jonathan, unsure if she had heard him correctly. Vic's friends and the music seemed to be getting louder by the minute, even with the door closed to his bedroom. He couldn't make eye contact, so he focused on the autographed Deion Sanders jersey that hung on the wall instead. At that moment, he appeared vulnerable and sweet. Her heart went out to him, and she was extremely relieved and flattered that he'd finally revealed the big mystery to her. Case solved.

"Thank you for sharing that. I was afraid you weren't attracted enough to me ..." she began.

He held up a hand to stop her. "Whoa! Hold it right there! Of course I'm attracted to you! You're the hottest, sexiest girl on the planet. I feel terrible you've been thinking that way!"

She shrugged, her eyes welling with tears. "How could I not? Whenever we would make out, or things began to heat up, you pushed me away."

He hung his head. "I'm so sorry, babe."

She scooted closer to him on the bed, placing her finger under his chin to turn his face toward her. The tears in his eyes surprised her, and she was deeply touched. He removed his glasses, and she gently dabbed his cheek. "Please don't cry. It's okay."

"No, it's not. I'm a grown man holding out for marriage. But I should have been just waiting for the right girl. And here she is, sitting right next to me! You're the answer to my prayers, so why can't I throw caution to the wind and make love to you?"

"I think it's because you simply want to wait until marriage. It's a spiritual decision, I'm guessing, and you would be so disappointed if you went back on your word with God."

Giving her hand a squeeze, he looked at her with admiration. "Has anyone ever told you you're a wise woman?"

She smiled. "Yes, all the time." She paused a moment, then continued.

"We really haven't been dating that long. Even if you were to change your mind, in which case God would understand, it might be best for your first time to be with someone you've been dating longer than three months!"

He placed his hand on the back of her neck to bring her closer to him. Ever so lightly, his lips brushed hers, and then he kissed the tip of her nose.

"I knew after our first date you were the one."

"Really?"

"Absolutely! Anyone who can be as beautiful as you while having a big heart and loving attitude is the girl for me."

She laughed but he didn't.

"I'm not kidding. *You* are the girl of my dreams. Most likely I will propose to you when I get my master's. We can be engaged while I'm working on my doctorate. I mean, we can't raise a family on my income from Chili's."

She nodded. "You're right. Okay, I can wait."

"There's a sparkle in your eyes, as if you think I'm teasing. I'm not."

The door was opened suddenly, and a couple entered who obviously wanted the room for the same reason they had.

"Oh! Sorry," the young man exclaimed. "We thought this room was empty."

Patience winked. "It's about to be."

* * *

"I forgot to give Tricia my phone number and say good bye." Patience opened the car door, but Jonathan stopped her.

"Why don't you just wait until we see her next time?"

"I promised I'd call her tomorrow so we can make plans for next weekend. We're going to start hanging out together."

He rolled his eyes. "But I'm ready to go. Besides, I don't want you to get closer to her. I need you all to myself." He kissed her cheek tenderly.

She giggled. "Sweetheart, you already see me more than Jana and Cole do. And they're my best friends!"

"Fine, but Tricia only gets Wednesdays. No weekends!"

As Patience reentered Vic's living room, she noticed that the crowd had begun to dwindle. She could walk through the house without being stepped on or pushed, which was a huge relief. The volume of the music was lower, and many of the guests were sitting quietly on couches and barstools, or on the floor, talking quietly and drinking. A couple who looked fifteen years of age was making out on the stairs, and a few guys were shooting pool in the den. She quickened her steps, anxious to find

Tricia so she could get back to Jonathan, who had decided to stay in the car.

She walked through the kitchen, catching sight of Vic on the patio out back. He was standing with a group of friends near the pool, his arm draped around yet a different girl's shoulders. Patience smiled, wondering just how many girlfriends this guy had. She decided to join them in the backyard, figuring Tricia was probably with the group. It was dimly lit, and she squinted before identifying Matt, Gerald, and Braxton sitting on lawn chairs. There were a handful of Vic's buddies whom she recognized, and they burst into laughter at something Matt said.

Feeling suddenly shy, she tiptoed on the patio in the dark, wondering if she should interrupt. No one noticed her, so she stood near the door, still as a statue.

"What do you call a black girl who thinks she's white?" Matt's voice boomed over the others' chatter.

"Oh, Matt, that's old! An Oreo," someone answered.

"Okay, okay, I got it! If the man is white and his girlfriend is black, is she really his slave?"

One of the guys snickered, and another one slapped Matt on the back. "You're reaching, man! Guess I'll give you an A for effort, though!"

Patience winced, feeling as if her entire body was numb.

The friend continued. "I've got one! Never trust mixed race people; they always have a dark side."

Matt stood, his shoulders squared and his chin held high. "Hey, man, I'm not sure I like that one. It's degrading to black people."

The guy shrugged. "Yeah, I guess you're right."

Matt snickered. "What's black and white and red all over? An interracial couple in a car wreck."

Everyone paused, and one of the girls rose to leave. "This is horrible. I can't stand listening to this crap." She turned swiftly on her heels and went inside. She didn't see Patience, who hovered in the corner of the patio, hidden by the darkness.

Vic shook his head. "Man, you need to cut that out. I'm not tolerating any hate in my house."

Matt laughed. "This ain't your house. It's your parents'."

"Just shut up!" Vic took a step closer to him. "Personally, I'm sick of your crap. You have a huge chip on your shoulder and love to put people down. I'm not taking it anymore."

Patience backed away slowly, bumping into the glass door before turning and running back into Vic's. She could barely see as the tears fell freely, her heart pounding so hard she wondered if a heart attack was coming. She sprinted out the front and down the sidewalk to the safety of Jonathan's car. Huge sobs began to overtake her as she slumped into the seat.

"Babe! What the hell?" He immediately pulled her into his arms. It took her a couple of minutes to regain her composure before she pulled back slightly to look at him. She told him the jokes she had overheard Matt telling everyone.

"What?" His eyes were as wide as saucers. "Are you sure?"

"Am I sure? Of course I am! Jonathan!" Here he was, doing it again. Sometimes he acted as if she wasn't hearing or seeing things correctly when Matt was involved.

"I'm just saying ..."

"What *are* you saying?" she pressed.

Brushing a tear that dangled on the tip of her chin, he sighed. "I have no idea, to tell the truth. I am so sorry for what you overheard. Matt is crazy, and I'm confronting him in the morning."

"It *is* morning."

"You know what I mean."

She opened his glove compartment in search of a Kleenex. She hadn't seen this coming and was surprised the night had ended so badly. Never before had she walked in on a racist joke fest. Sure, in the past she'd overheard a couple of teenagers saying Patience thought she was white. And yes, Tripp's parents had once decorated their picnic table with Aunt Jemima's face and also prepared food that they figured black people would like, such as fried chicken with hot sauce, sweet potatoes and greens. Tripp had been livid, really letting his parents have it that day. His mother didn't like African-Americans and didn't want her son dating one.

Yet tonight, when Patience had heard those cruel jokes, she'd felt as if someone had slapped her or punched her in the stomach. Matt couldn't stand her just because she was mixed. The fact that he tried to bring others into his hate-filled world made things worse. On top of that, insinuating that Sharise was John's slave instead of his wife brought her blood to a boil. Sitting in Jonathan's car, wondering when he would decide what his next move would be, she felt nauseous. She wanted him to storm into Vic's and throttle Matt's neck until he pleaded for mercy. More than that, she wished she didn't have to tell him to do it.

"Are we going to sit here till Monday?" she asked sarcastically. Fastening her seat belt, her eyes remained on the streetlight ahead.

"No, I guess not." He started the care but didn't drive off.

"What do you want me to do?" he asked as he turned in the seat to face her.

Swallowing the lump in her throat, she closed her eyes. "Nothing."

"Should I go back in there and confront him?"

"Nah, just take me home."

"Patience, please don't be mad at me." His words were shaky.

She opened her eyes but couldn't bring herself to face him. She stared out the window instead.

"Sweetheart," he pleaded, "please understand my predicament. Matt is my best friend. We're brothers. I love him. Now, that doesn't mean I agree with what he's saying, obviously. He's being a closed-minded jerk! And he will have to answer to me. I care about you deeply, no matter what. You have to believe that!" He stopped suddenly, inhaling and exhaling slowly, as if to remain calm.

"Please look at me."

She blew her nose and then turned to him.

"Honestly, it would be nice if you went back in there to defend my honor, to show them that it is *not* okay to say those things." She shrugged. "Oh well, that's something you're going to have to pray about and work out with your conscience."

They sat in silence for a while, each lost in thought. And finally, to Patience's relief, Jonathan pulled away from the curb and drove her home.

Chapter 13

"You have got to be kidding me!" Jana exclaimed, her dark brown eyes almost popping out of her head.

"Nope," Patience replied softly, shivering slightly in the cool morning air.

The two sat on a bench at Rory's favorite park, taking a short break from their jog along the trail. After tossing and turning in bed, Patience had given up on her quest for sleep, deciding to wake Jana at eight. Being the true friend Patience loved, Jana had been at her house by eight thirty, and they'd needed the exercise to release the anger dwelling in their bodies. Rory laid near their feet chewing the grass and then choking on it. A father pushed his toddler twins in the swings on the playground, while a couple of ducks waddled next to the small lake nearby, stopping momentarily to look at Rory. However, the dog didn't move, as the jog had worn him out. There weren't many people out that chilly morning. Patience guessed they were either sleeping in or at church, where she should've been.

Jana tightened her ponytail, clearly irritated. "What did he say when y'all made it home?"

"Neither of us said a word. I got out of the car without

125

kissing him or anything. He did make sure I got in safely before driving off, but I haven't heard from him."

"Girl, you need to break up with him and his friends."

"I can't. I'm in like with him."

Jana laughed. "You mean love."

She shook her head. "It's almost love but not quite. Probably in another month or so, it will be, though."

"You are so weird!"

"I know."

The girls stood, and Jana picked up Rory's leash to lead him back toward the trail. She exhaled loudly. "I'm pooped."

Patience nodded. "I am, too. I'm drained emotionally and physically. Let's just walk once more around the park and then we can call it quits. I'm not ready to go home yet."

"I understand. Maybe you can hang out at my house for a bit. We should rent movies or go shopping. We need to get your mind off of this."

As they strolled down the trail, the events of the past week swirled around Patience's mind, leaving her bewildered.

"What bothers me the most is Jonathan's lack of involvement in this whole fiasco. He gets upset when I tell him about it, but he doesn't say anything. I want him to stand up for me."

"I agree one hundred percent. Besides, Matt isn't the only person who's going to say rude things to you. Jonathan better be prepared to fight for you at least once a week."

"Once a week? Dang! I don't encounter these situations that often!"

Rory caught sight of a bird and began barking wildly, threatening to break free from Jana's grasp.

"Calm down, Rory! You know you're scared of birds, anyway," Jana reminded him as she tried to pull him back to her.

"Do you want me to get him?" Patience offered.

"Nah, I can handle him. Anyway, Jonathan needs a backbone. Matt is like a brother to him, but who cares? Wrong is wrong. He better stand up to him or he might lose you."

"Mmhmm. Another question popped into my head this morning. Jonathan looks biracial. So how in the world did those two end up friends in the first place?"

"You're absolutely right! He resembles you, actually."

"Yep, he sure does! I guess Matt approves of people who appear mixed but aren't. As long as both parents are of the same race, they're not breaking his law."

The two laughed as they turned and headed to Patience's house.

* * *

That evening, Jonathan called to ask what her plans were for Thanksgiving, which was the following Thursday.

Patience gasped. "Oh my goodness, I forgot all about it! And it's my favorite holiday!" She stood in her kitchen making pancakes for dinner, the butterflies returning to her tummy at the sound of his voice. It was only seven p.m., but she had her pajamas on. She was exhausted and planned on going to bed extremely early. She was happy they had a short workweek, a perk to being a high school teacher. Cole had sent her a text earlier that afternoon inviting her over to his family's feast. Every year she spent time with him, his parents, and his younger brother Stephen.

127

"My mom reminded me today. I went by to visit, and she told me to bring you with me."

"Aww, that is so sweet! Your parents are awesome," she praised, flipping the pancake with the spatula and watching it fall to the floor. "Crap!"

"What is it?"

"My dinner just fell, and Rory's on his way to clean it up."

Jonathan chuckled. "He wants to help any way he can!"

Patience popped a strawberry in her mouth, opening the fridge to grab some eggs.

"So, how was your day?" he asked.

"I can't complain. And yours?"

"It went pretty well."

As she prepared the batter yet again, she felt brave enough to abandon the small talk and discuss the elephant in the room.

"Did you get a chance to chat with Matt?"

"Um, not yet, but I will."

She poured the batter into the skillet. "Why not?"

He stalled. "Well ... I texted him this morning, but he hasn't responded."

"Oh."

Changing the subject, he said, "My parents usually eat Thanksgiving dinner at around noon, so I can pick you up at eleven if you like."

"I'll let you know by tomorrow. I have to see what time Cole wants me over, as well as my family."

"That sounds good. I'll talk to you tomorrow, then." He hesitated and then added, "I missed seeing you today."

She wanted to answer *whatever* but didn't feel like getting into an argument.

"I missed you, too," she replied instead.

"Are we okay?"

She took a sip of her milk, sitting down at the table with her breakfast for dinner. The unmistakable feeling of nausea from the night before began to return.

"Yes, we are."

Chapter 14

"And Lord, please bless this food we are about to receive for the nourishment of our bodies. Amen."

Everyone sang *Amen* in unison, opening their eyes with delight as they stared at the scrumptious desserts before them. Patience thought she'd died and gone to Heaven. Pumpkin and sweet potato pie, coconut cake, and homemade cinnamon rolls were to the left of her. Chocolate cake, apple cobbler, and pumpkin bread were on her right. Cliff Brown held the huge bowl of Watergate salad for a few seconds before his wife playfully swatted his hand.

"Honey, put that down this minute. I think we need to go around the table and have everyone name something they're thankful for."

Lily Brown rolled her eyes. "Aww, man! Mom, we've waited all day for this moment! If I don't get a taste of pie this instant, I'll die!"

Patience laughed, amused by the desperation painted on the teen's face. Jonathan's sister was so cute, very dramatic and extremely friendly. Patience was impressed by how smart and quick-witted Lily was. She could see now why Jonathan and his parents were so proud of her.

"Stop whining," her big brother ordered, resting his elbows on the table. "You've waited this long, so an extra two minutes won't kill ya."

Patricia nodded. "I agree."

The five of them sat in the cozy dining room that Thanksgiving evening, each one grateful for many things. Patience hadn't been able to come over any earlier than three o'clock, as the McKlendons had their feast at one. Sharise would have strangled her daughter if she'd missed it. To compromise, Jonathan's family promised to hold off on dessert until later. Cole was expecting her at six, so she had plenty of time.

Cliff went first. "I'm thankful for my family."

Patricia smiled, reaching across the table to hold her husband's hand.

"Where do I begin? I am so grateful for my family and friends, as well as my relationship with God, my health, the roof over my head-"

Lily sighed impatiently.

Her mother shrugged. "Sorry, I guess I'm thankful for everything."

Jonathan smiled. "I thank God for His mercy, and for my family, as well. Also, I am so blessed to have found the love of my life."

Patience felt her lower lip quiver, but she kept her composure. Clearing her throat, she sat up straighter, her eyes meeting his. "I'm thankful for you, Jonathan, and for my family and friends. I could go on, but I don't want Lily to faint from sugar deprivation."

Everyone laughed.

"It's okay," Lily reassured. "I like you so you're good. By the

132

way, I am very thankful to be out of school for a few days. Pass the pumpkin pie, please!"

* * *

"Patience, we're thrilled you were able to come today. Jonathan talks about you constantly. And frankly, we can see why. You're such a lovely young lady," Patricia praised. She took a sip of her coffee, a twinkle in her soft brown eyes. She was a pretty woman, tall and slender, with only a hint of gray sprinkled in her black hair. Although their skin tones were different, Jonathan resembled her quite a bit. They had the same nose and wide grin, and both exuded charm and warmth. Patience felt very relaxed with the Browns, who were so open and loving.

Cliff nodded, adding more marshmallows to his hot chocolate. "My Patty's right. It's not often that Jonathan brings a girl over to spend time with us, so that means you're pretty special." He winked at his son. "You did well."

"You all are going to make me cry," she admitted, feeling her throat tighten. In the recent past, only Roman's parents had been this accepting of her, able to see past the color of her skin and enjoy getting to know her as a person. So she didn't want to take this for granted. The fact that she was welcome in their home to have the opportunity to bond with them was a blessing.

Cliff chuckled. "Well, we certainly don't want that! Let's steer the conversation in a different direction, shall we?"

Everyone smiled.

"That's a good idea, sweetheart," Patricia agreed. "So, tell us what you love most about teaching."

133

Jonathan walked Patience to her car, his arm around her waist as he glanced up at the sky.

"The only thing I don't like about the fall is that it gets dark so early. I feel like I should be in bed right now."

"You are so right! It makes me tired just being out here," she agreed.

The two laughed as a familiar BMW pulled up to the Browns' curb. Patience felt her heart sink at the sight of Matt's vehicle.

I should have left five minutes ago, she thought in despair.

"I better go," she said quickly, standing on her tiptoes to give Jonathan a kiss on his forehead. "I had a wonderful time! Thanks so much for inviting me over." Her hands trembled slightly as she dug in her purse for her keys.

"Don't leave yet," he responded, his arm tightening around her.

"What's up, buddy?" Matt yelled out the car window. Jonathan walked over to greet him, practically dragging her along.

"Hey! Happy Thanksgiving!"

Patience stood with her arms folded across her chest. She wondered if she should speak or stand there like an idiot. What she wanted to do was leave, as Cole and his parents were expecting her. She didn't feel like making small talk and knew Matt didn't, either.

"We all just finished having dessert. There's plenty in there, so help yourself."

His friend joined them on the sidewalk, his hands thrust in the pockets of his jeans.

"I will! Your mom called last night to make sure I was coming over today. She's so sweet."

Unable to tolerate being ignored, Patience disengaged herself from Jonathan's grasp and headed to her car.

"I'll see you inside," she heard Matt say. Jonathan was next to her in seconds. She unlocked the door and got in without looking at him.

"What's wrong?" he asked as she started the ignition.

"Everything is fine. I love it when people are rude to me."

He opened the door, squatting so he was at her level. "Matt was in a hurry to see my parents and get to those desserts." He laughed awkwardly.

She put the car in reverse. "I don't care what he does or the reasons he does it."

"Patience!"

She paused. "Look, I haven't brought it up since Sunday, but it bothers me that you haven't mentioned the incident anymore."

"What incident?"

She decided to let it go. If they got into a heated discussion about telling racist jokes now, she would be late meeting Cole. And she didn't want her best friend mad at her again. Ever since she'd forgotten the plans they had made a while back, their relationship was slightly rocky. He'd called a few times to chat, but there was an unmistakable friction in the air, and she was determined to make things right. Besides, Jonathan was acting as if he didn't know what she was talking about, and she didn't have all night to refresh his memory.

She sighed. "I'll call you tonight when I get home."

"But ..."

"Sweetie, I'm going to be late. I promise I will call you later."

He stood quickly, pouting like a child. "All right, I guess I have no choice. Have fun with Cole."

* * *

As it turned out, Patience was fifteen minutes late.

"I'm so sorry, Cate!" she apologized as she stepped into the Mendezes' home.

Cole's mother hugged her tight. "Don't be silly! We're so glad you came! Come in, come in!"

At five feet two inches, Cate had to look up when talking to almost everyone. She was thin, with short, blonde hair and blue eyes, and she appeared to be much younger than her forty-eight years of age. She also acted young, always having an abundance of energy and a perky disposition. She was the total opposite of Cole's father, Robert, who was six feet tall, dark, and handsome. Cole inherited all his features from his dad, who was Cuban. His brother Steven took after Cate. He could have easily passed for white if he wanted to. However, like Cole, he was proud to be mixed with Cuban and white. They were a beautiful family, both inside and out.

"Patience! How's my future daughter-in-law?" Cole's dad came in and took her in his arms. Ever since she and Cole were kids, both sets of parents predicted and hoped they would be married by the time they were thirty.

"I'm doing great! Sorry I'm late."

Robert Mendez waved a hand dismissively. "You are welcome here anytime! Sweetheart, we would wait until three a.m. for you.

"Now," he continued in a more serious tone, "what is this I hear about you dating some fellow named Jonathan? Cole tells me the young man is not good enough for you, and I agree, even though I haven't met him."

"Dad!" Cole's voice came from the den, and he emerged seconds later, his dark hair sticking straight up all over his head.

She laughed. "What happened? Did you get struck by lightning?"

Cate laughed as well. "He's doing some repair work for me since I can't get anyone else to do it." She shot her husband a meaningful look. "What was the excuse you used this time? You're sick, right?"

Robert reached around to rub the back of his neck, pretending to be in pain.

"No, honey, remember I told you my neck was sore from exercising yesterday?"

Cate began walking to the kitchen. "By exercise he means getting up to change the channel on the television manually. We lost the remote."

She motioned for Patience to follow her, and the women caught up on old times as they reheated turkey and dressing from earlier. She almost gagged at the sight of all the food. She was stuffed. There was no way she could eat another dinner. She was going to have just a tiny bit of turkey and a scoop of cranberry sauce, but that was it. Otherwise, she would be hugging the toilet all night.

The men joined them in the dining area shortly afterward, and everyone was in good spirits as they ate. Patience asked about Steven, who was spending most of the day with his new girlfriend and her family.

Robert cleared his throat dramatically. "Okay, young lady, you're not getting off that easily. I want to know everything about this new guy you're seeing. What does he do for a living? How old is he? Does he have a college degree? Where does he live? Is he saved? If so, what church does he attend? And finally, when are you two breaking up?"

She was taking a huge gulp of her Sprite when his father began spewing all the questions about her love life. The soda went down the wrong pipe when she giggled, causing her to choke. As she coughed uncontrollably, Cole jumped up to pat her on the back.

"Are you okay?"

Finally catching her breath, she smiled at her friend with tears in her eyes. "Oh, sure, I'm fine."

Robert clapped his hands. "What a relief! Now, does Jonathan work?"

Cate swatted at her husband. "Where are your manners? Patience is over there almost dying, and you're playing *Twenty Questions*."

"No, no, I'm good." Wiping her tears with a napkin, she filled them in on Jonathan's statistics.

"... and we have so much fun together," she finished, a frown forming on her lips.

The Mendez family fell silent, watching her closely while they ate. Patience began toying with her turkey, stabbing it with the fork and then pulling each piece apart slowly.

Robert pushed his plate to the side, leaning forward and resting his elbows on the table. His dark brown eyes studied her.

"Hmm, I hear what you're saying. Unfortunately, your body language doesn't match your words."

"Yeah, Dad, I agree. Something's not right." Cole reached over to pat her hand. "What is it?"

She shrugged. "Nothing ..." She started to deny that anything was wrong but couldn't do it. Even if she were able to finish the sentence, they wouldn't believe her. This family had known her since she was a child, and they had the skills to see right through her. However, she didn't want to cry in front of them, especially on Thanksgiving. And Cate was such a worry-wart. She'd most likely lose sleep if she found out a man was mistreating her.

"Let's just say that his friend and I don't get along, which is causing friction in my relationship with Jonathan."

Cole sat up straighter. "How can anyone not get along with you? You're perfect."

She smiled. "Thanks, Coley. This friend of his is like a brother to him. They grew up together and are tight. They made a pact that if one of them didn't like the other's girlfriend, he would dump her."

Cate's mouth dropped open. "That's the stupidest thing I've ever heard. What should it matter if his friend doesn't get along with you?"

"Is his friend crazy?" Robert cut in. "What excuse does he give for not liking the sweetest, most endearing girl in Texas?"

She pushed a lock of hair off her shoulders. "You all put me on a pedestal. I'm flattered. Sadly, Matt can't stand me because I'm mixed."

Cole's eyes narrowed. "He told you that?"

She nodded. "When I first met him, he was really rude and

139

obnoxious. I couldn't figure out what it was about me that irked him. Then one night he made a remark that people should stay with their own kind. He made it known he is against interracial dating and doesn't like anyone who is biracial. And the other night, I overheard him telling racist jokes to his friends about people who are mixed."

Cate's blue eyes widened, her pale face turning crimson. Robert stood and began pacing back and forth through the dining room.

"I can't believe this. *I cannot believe what I am hearing*! See what this world is coming to? I tell ya, we're in the last days. Don't I keep telling you that, Cate? Ah, the ignorance of some never ceases to amaze me! Damn!" He ran a hand through his hair in frustration, pausing a moment to gaze at his family. "This may be the twenty-first century, but I swear, sometimes it feels like we're still living in the dark ages. It nauseates me!"

Cole glared at her. "What does Jonathan say about all this?"

"He acts as if I'm blowing things out of proportion. He either ignores Matt or tells me to think positive, that he'll come around eventually."

"So what you're saying is Jonathan thinks it's okay to be a bigot," Robert hissed.

Patience could feel her face burning, and she needed some fresh air to clear her head. "Jonathan is not siding with him. He's caught between a rock and a hard place. He doesn't know how to handle this. He cares for both me and Matt. He told me he can't risk losing either of us."

"You've got to be kidding me," Cate said. Rising from her seat, she walked over to sit beside Patience, taking her hand.

"Sweetie, I hurt for you. I know this is a tough situation,

but trust me. Things will only get worse. Jonathan is tolerating Matt's horrible behavior, showing him that it is okay to treat you with disrespect. You need to have a long talk with him as soon as possible. Tell him you won't put up with this nonsense."

"I will."

Cole scoffed. "Are you sure? How long has this been going on, anyway?"

Her eyes were downcast. "I'm not sure."

"That's bullshit."

"Cole! Watch your mouth," his mother scolded.

"I'm sorry, Mom, but I can't stand when Patience is too nice for her own good. This has probably been going on since she met that a*hole!"

"I told you I can't remember!" she cried, standing to leave the room.

Robert approached her, concern evident on his face. "Please don't think we're ganging up on you. We love you and are very overprotective. To find out someone, *anyone*, is treating you badly hurts us. You're like a daughter to me, and I can't suppress the anger inside me tonight. I'm certain Cate and Cole are feeling the same."

Patience hugged him first and then Cate. Cole stood seething nearby.

"Excuse me," he said as he left the dining room in a huff.

Chapter 15

Patience followed Cole, her heart heavy in her chest. This was by far the worst holiday she'd ever had. Grabbing her sweater off the couch, she met him in the backyard. Although it was November, the weather was still too warm for a heavy coat. She watched him pick up a handful of tiny rocks off the ground and walk to the edge of the pool. He began throwing them in the water, his back to her. She sat on a patch of cool grass, and the two were silent for a while. She took a deep breath of the night air, her body finally beginning to relax slightly. Fireflies danced around her, their lights flickering on and off as she savored the change of scenery. It had been way too intense in the Mendezes' house, thanks to her.

Shaking her head, she tried to erase the images of the family's disappointed looks from her mind. She should have kept her mouth shut about Jonathan, or at least tried to work it out herself before bringing others into the drama.

"Are you upset with me?" she asked softly.

He didn't turn around. "No, I'm not. I do have a bone to pick with your so-called boyfriend, however."

"Believe it or not, he's a good guy. I know that sounds crazy, after everything I've told you about his friend-"

"You're right about that," he interrupted.

He turned on his heel and approached quickly, plopping himself down on the grass next to her. Reaching up to tuck the stray curl behind her ear, he frowned.

"Patience, I'm horrified that you allow this kind of treatment. Jonathan may not have control over his friend's beliefs, but one thing is certain. He needs to stand up for you. He should confront Matt and tell him he may *not* ridicule or behave badly toward you. It's the right thing to do. By remaining silent, he's giving him the go-ahead to act a fool."

She nodded. "I know."

He put an arm around her and pulled her close. "I know you know. That's the irritating part. You're an intelligent woman. Act like one."

* * *

Patience arrived home at midnight, her arms filled with leftover goodies for Rory. Cate adored him and always sent treats his way. After dumping the scraps of turkey into his bowl, she quickly showered and took an Advil. Due to the stressful night, she could feel a slight headache coming. She couldn't stand this predicament. Although she adored Jonathan and wanted this relationship to work, her gut told her trouble was brewing. Cole was right. As her boyfriend, Jonathan's natural instinct should have been to stand up for her. At the restaurant, when Matt had made the comment about interracial dating, Jonathan should have told him to shut up. And when she'd returned to his car in tears the night of the party, Jonathan should have marched back in there and punched his lights out. But no, she had to beg him just to talk to his friend.

As she climbed into bed, she felt angry, sad, and frustrated simultaneously. She reached for her cell to text Jonathan good night. She didn't have the emotional strength to talk to him at that moment. He responded immediately, asking if he could call her. She wrote back that she was exhausted and that they could chat in the morning. She had plans to go shopping with her mother and Jana for Black Friday, but she also knew it was important to talk to him. Pulling the covers higher, she sank into bed and closed her heavy eyelids, praying that sweet slumber would come soon.

* * *

The next morning, Jonathan was very defensive and moody during their conversation. Patience called him as soon as she woke up, feeling refreshed and anxious to start the day. Before she'd fallen asleep, Cole's advice had kept running through her mind over and over: *You're an intelligent woman. Act like one.* She knew she deserved to be treated with respect. She was a good person, always trying her best not to hurt others and show them grace. It wouldn't hurt Jonathan to confront his friend about his undesirable behavior.

"So when exactly are you going to talk to Matt?"

He sighed heavily into the phone. "How many times are you going to ask me that?"

Immediately her pulse quickened. "Um, I guess fifty."

She tried to laugh but coughed instead.

Silence.

"Are you there?" she asked, entering her closet to find something casual to wear.

He cleared his throat. "Am I going to see you today? How long are y'all going to be shopping?"

She rolled her eyes. "Unfortunately, we'll probably be out most of the day. I can't stand shopping. We can hang out tonight if you want. And then we can discuss Matt ..."

"Gosh, will you give it a rest? I told you I haven't had a chance to bring up the biracial subject yet."

"Jonathan! What is wrong with you? The only reason I keep pestering is because I feel like you're ignoring me."

"How can I ignore something you keep nagging me about?"

She drew in a deep breath, hurt by his sharp tone. The doorbell interrupted the silence that had descended upon them. She was thankful for the excuse to let him go.

"I bet that's Jana at the door. I need to leave."

He sighed. "All right, if you still feel like seeing me later, Braxton's having a couple of us over to watch the game. He wanted me to invite you."

"Sure, that sounds like fun," she answered in a flat voice. The excitement she used to experience at the prospect of spending time with Jonathan was gone. She did care about him, but lately his loyalty was to Matt. As she tossed a couple of dog treats into Rory's bowl, Patience tried to think positive. She liked Braxton and Vic, and she loved watching football. Perhaps Tricia would be there, too. The night could turn out to be fun.

"Go, Cowboys!" Braxton shouted from his seat in the living room. Everyone laughed, as Braxton was the shy one of the group. In the time she had known him, Patience had never heard him raise his voice or act excited about anything. However, this game seemed to bring out his extrovert side. Gerald and Vic stood cheering like maniacs, along with a couple of their other friends. Patience jumped up, as well, almost knocking over the bowl of popcorn on the coffee table in front of her. Jonathan clapped loudly, pride for his favorite team obvious by the huge grin on his face. Only Matt frowned, as he was rooting for the Seahawks.

Patience was disappointed Tricia hadn't come. Matt said she'd stayed home, sick with the flu. There were other girls at Braxton's, yet she hadn't gotten to know any of them. Gerald's girlfriend seemed really sweet, but the opportunity to chat with her hadn't surfaced. Vic hadn't brought anyone with him that night, which was a surprise to everyone. He joked that he was waiting for a girl like Patience to show up in his life, which pissed Jonathan off tremendously. He'd been in a horrible mood when he'd picked her up earlier, and Vic's comment made matters worse. When the Cowboys made a touchdown, he finally smiled.

"I'm going to the restroom," she told him after the cheering died down. A couple of the guys went to the kitchen for more drinks, and they smiled at her as they passed.

He nodded. "Okay."

As she entered Braxton's hallway, she noticed Matt behind her. Immediately she felt goose bumps pop up on her arms, so she quickened her pace.

Suddenly he called out to her. She stopped, turning around slowly to find him standing with his arms folded, his chin held high, and his posture perfectly straight. He reeked of arrogance, and it almost hurt to look at him.

She tried to smile. "Yes?"

"What do you call five hundred thousand white guys who jump out of a plane?"

He didn't know Vic had just entered the hallway and was standing behind him, waiting for the response.

She squared her shoulders, trying her best to appear more confident than she felt. Her lips remained shut. She knew another racist joke was on its way.

Matt smirked. "Snowfall."

Her green eyes flashed, and she took a step closer to him, her hands clenched into fists at her sides. "Why you ..." she began, but he held up his hands to stop her.

"Hey, you're biracial. Shouldn't you only be half offended?"

Suddenly, Vic grabbed Matt from behind by his collar and yanked him to the ground. Both were very strong, but Vic had height on him. And rage. Matt gasped for air as Vic straddled him, his white cheeks red from anger. Vic had Matt's entire body pinned down, and for once, Matt was vulnerable. Vic punched him in the face, and Patience screamed. She bent over the two, her arms going around Vic's waist to pull him off of Matt, but it was like trying to move the Incredible Hulk. As a matter of fact, he reminded her of the superhero with the tortured soul. He was sweet as pie until one pushed him to the limit, unleashing the anger that had once lain dormant in his soul.

"*I want you out of this house immediately*!" Vic commanded. "*You racist bastard*!"

After hearing the commotion, the others came running into the hallway, led by Braxton.

"What the ... ?" Jonathan exclaimed, rushing to help Gerald and Braxton pull Vic off of him.

"What is this all about?" Braxton huffed, already out of breath just from containing Vic. It took four guys to rescue Matt. Vic was extremely fit and muscular. Plus, anger had the ability to make even the weakest person strong and dangerous.

Patience filled them in on the words spoken right before the attack. Gerald shook his head, while Jonathan's mouth hung open in shock.

Matt wiped the beads of sweat dripping down his forehead. "He's crazy! I was joking around, that's all. And he tried to kill me!"

A few of their friends stood up for Matt.

"We all know he jokes about race. No big deal. Why is everyone so sensitive, anyway?"

"Yeah, whatever happened to freedom of speech?"

"Violence never solves anything," Gerald's girlfriend added.

Vic pointed a finger at Matt, his voice steady and firm as he said, "I have put up with your rudeness and your hateful ways long enough. We are no longer friends. And if I *ever* hear about you harassing Patience, or anyone else, I will finish what I started tonight!"

To her surprise, Matt didn't say anything. He waited until Vic stormed off before retreating to Braxton's bedroom.

* * *

Fifteen minutes later, things had settled, and most of the guests were acting as if nothing out of the ordinary had happened. The football game was still going strong, and Gerald opened the door for the pizza-delivery guy. Braxton seemed to revert back to being an introvert, his eyes glazed over as he watched the game. A couple of the guys Patience didn't know were drinking beer as they played cards in the dining room. She glanced at the clock above the mantle, wondering how much longer before they could leave. Jonathan hadn't said a word since both Vic and Matt had left. At this point, she couldn't care less.

Leaning toward him, she whispered, "I'm ready to go home."

"Let's go, then," he replied, his face void of emotion.

After saying good bye to everyone and thanking Braxton for having them over, Patience and Jonathan left. As they climbed into his car, neither said a word. She was disappointed beyond belief, and nothing he said would make her feel better. And although it saddened her, she knew it was good to find out who he felt more loyal to. She could never compete with Matt, his best friend for so long.

He pulled into her driveway but left the car running. Turning to her, he looked defeated. Before he could say anything, she placed her hand on his, smiling sadly in the dark car.

"I guess this is it. I now see how important Matt is to you. And that's okay. I understand, and I want you to know that I will always care about you."

He frowned. "If I didn't know any better, I'd say you were breaking up with me."

Her mouth dropped open. That was exactly what she was doing. Yet he seemed dumbfounded.

She sat back in the seat. "I'm sorry. I assumed we were through. Matt has been the biggest jerk to me, and the only one standing up for me is Vic. What are your thoughts about this? To be honest, I can't endure his tasteless jokes, evil stares, and hateful comments any longer."

"Babe, I'm so sorry. I promise I won't allow this to happen again. It has spiraled out of control, I know. And I'm the only one to blame. But please don't leave me! We can work it out."

She shook her head, her eyes filling with tears. "You said that last time, and the time before that. Your words are not matching your actions. And even if you *do* say something to him, you will end up resenting me, especially if you lose his friendship as a result."

Running a hand through his hair, he sat up straighter, his voice shaky. "It doesn't have to be this way. I can keep my relationship with both of you. He'll change. He has to."

She knew he was speaking out of desperation now. "You can't force someone to change. He believes what he wants to believe. Maybe he was raised that way. Who knows? But I will not come between you and him anymore. I'm willing to let you go."

"Don't let me go! Please, Patience, I'm begging you. I can't lose you. Give me one more chance!"

To her dismay, Jonathan started crying. She moved closer to wrap her arms around him, kissing him softly on his cheek. Her heart softened as she held him, touched by the remorse he felt about the situation. Maybe he had issues with confrontation just as she did. Matt's aggressive nature made it hard for anyone to stand up to him, she was sure of it. She couldn't fault Jonathan for being unable to do something she herself couldn't do. And as the two sat in the car, Patience was more confused than ever. She didn't know what to do.

Chapter 16

The first week of December was hectic for Patience. Between catching up on lesson plans, Christmas shopping, and volunteering at her church by helping with childcare, she barely had time to breathe. Sister Camden, the head of the Mission and Social Action Committee, also talked her into assisting with their annual holiday fair, which donated the proceeds to various homeless shelters in Dallas. She also tried spending as much time as she could with her parents, Cole, Jana, and Jonathan. Although their relationship was shaky, she and Jonathan were making a huge effort to strengthen it. She cared for him so deeply and knew he felt the same for her.

After the Matt/Vic incident, the couple had steered clear of parties and get-togethers, choosing instead to go out alone or with his family. They couldn't visit *her* parents or friends because no one cared to be around him. John and Sharise refused to invite him over, unable to believe Patience was still seeing him. John insisted that Jonathan was as guilty as Matt for allowing his friend to disrespect her. Cole threatened to beat him to a pulp, and Jana bought her several self-help books on unhealthy relationships and addiction recovery.

"I am not addicted to him," she whined one night to her

friend on the phone. "I just don't believe in throwing in the towel so soon. We'll work it out."

Jana scoffed. "He's manipulating you, girl! What else has to happen before you finally get it? His number-one priority is Matt. You come second. All he wants to do is sleep with you, and then he's gone."

"That's not true! He loves me, I can tell!"

"Ha! Get a clue, Patience. I'll bet he's not a virgin. He plays on your sympathy. He knows how naïve and sweet you are. Trust me. The guy's a jerk, and his friend is a racist jerk. They probably laugh at you when you're not around."

"Why are you saying these nasty things?" She choked the words out between sobs. "You're supposed to be my friend."

"I *am*, and that's why I'm willing to risk making you mad by telling the truth. Someone has to enlighten you."

By the end of the conversation, Patience was worn out. Everywhere she turned, someone gave her hell about Jonathan. She had no one on her side. Even Rory's behavior had cooled toward her boyfriend, and he liked everyone. He no longer jumped up excitedly when Jonathan came over. Instead, the dog gazed up at him for a few seconds and then moved on to other things.

On Saturday afternoon, Patience decided to surprise Jonathan by baking Christmas cookies for him. They were his favorite holiday treat. After rolling out the sugar cookie dough, she found the cookie cutters in the top drawer. Carefully, she pressed the snowman-, candy cane-, and Christmas tree-shaped cutters into the dough. She wanted them to be perfect. When they were done, she placed them in one of the Christmas tins she'd purchased the day before, anxious to deliver them. She knew he would be home relaxing. They'd spoken the night before, and he'd told her he planned on watching college football and chilling. His roommate was out of town, so the timing was perfect.

The temperature had dropped significantly since Thanksgiving, and she put on a heavy coat as she hurried to the door. She wore a red turtleneck, jeans, and boots, and she had taken the time to straighten her hair, which fell just below her shoulders. She smiled to herself as she climbed into her car, giddy from the joy of doing something nice for him. The past few months had been stressful for them, yet she knew deep down that he was special. She couldn't wait to see the expression on his face when he opened the door. He would most likely take her in his arms and smother her with kisses, touched by the surprise.

She turned onto his street as tiny raindrops began to fall. The weatherman had announced that morning that there would be no rain, so she laughed as she turned on the windshield wipers.

"I could be a meteorologist," she whispered with a giggle, slowing down to enjoy the Christmas decorations in the yards. His house was at the very end of the long street, and when she was near, she blinked. There were six vehicles, including Matt's BMW, parked at Jonathan's. She maneuvered her car alongside the curb with a frown. He'd told her he would be alone that day, not that he needed her permission to have people over. An uneasy feeling crept up inside her as she sat for a moment, wondering what to do.

Pushing aside her doubts, Patience gathered her purse and his cookies, pulling her collar up higher as she exited the car. She hadn't driven all the way over for nothing. She wanted to see him, if only for a moment. She was his girlfriend, after all. She could invite herself in to his party, or gathering, if she chose to. If she ended up being the only girl there, that wouldn't be a problem. She would drop the cookies off, kiss him quickly, and leave.

The front door was ajar when she reached the porch. She shrugged, pushing it open and letting herself in. Gerald, Braxton, and one of the guys she'd seen at Braxton's the month before were sitting on the couch watching the game. She approached them slowly, suddenly hesitant about barging in on their fun. Gerald noticed her first. He jumped up to greet her.

"Patience! It's good to see you!" He hugged her distractedly, his focus still on the game.

She laughed. "Thanks, it's good to see you, too! Hi, Braxton!"

He got up to help her with her coat, draping it over a chair with care. "Hey, Patience, you're late. We've been here for a couple of hours already."

"I had no idea Jonathan was having everyone over today."

He raised an eyebrow. "Really? When I asked about you, he said you were sick."

"He did? I wonder why."

Braxton bit his lower lip, shifting his weight from one leg to the other. "Um, I don't know. You should ask him. He's in the kitchen with Matt."

She walked toward the kitchen, the uneasy feeling returning with full force. Reaching the doorway, she paused, the tin of cookies still in her hand.

"I'm telling you, Stacy wants you bad," Matt said, reaching into the bag of chips and stuffing a handful in his mouth.

Jonathan stirred the vegetable dip. "Will you please quit saying that? You know I'm taken."

His friend rolled his eyes. "You need to let that zebra go! She's nothing but trouble. Why not date a black woman?"

Jonathan looked up. "Patience is all I need. Now let's change the subject." He ripped open a bag of baby carrots and placed them on the tray.

Matt scowled. "I can't stand that witch. She's so sensitive. And what is she, anyway, black or white? Man! Mixed people get on my nerves. They get offended easily and ..."

Patience couldn't take it anymore. She burst into the kitchen, throwing the cookie tin across the room. Matt and Jonathan jumped as they turned and saw her. She stood with her hands on her hips, her hair beginning to curl slightly from the rain. Her mouth formed a line as she pressed her lips together tightly, and she could feel her cheeks burning, knowing that they were the color of scarlet, but she didn't care. She narrowed her eyes as she looked from one friend to the other, words escaping her for the moment. Her mind raced as she tried to make sense of everything. However, nothing made sense.

Finally, she found her voice. Pointing a finger at Jonathan, she said, "How *dare* you stand here and allow this ... this ... idiot to badmouth me. My father's right. You're just as much to blame as Matt! I can't believe this. I came over to surprise you because I treasured our relationship."

He took a step toward her, holding his arms out as his eyes moistened with unshed tears. "Sweetie ..."

She flinched. "Don't call me sweetie. I have nothing else to say to you, Jonathan. This is it. We're through!"

157

She fled from the kitchen, tears blinding her as she stumbled down the hall to get her coat. Braxton followed, full of concern and pity. Both he and Jonathan had to run to catch up with her. Braxton was out of breath when all three made it to her car, and Jonathan cried openly, his eyes puffy and red behind his glasses, his face stricken with pain. He was a good actor, standing there with his shoulders slumped as if he actually felt remorse. He was the epitome of heartache.

"Please, baby ..." he managed to say between gut-wrenching sobs. "I'll die if you leave me!"

Braxton approached her tentatively, reaching out to touch her shoulder. She stood with her back to them, ready to flee the scene. The dark clouds and light mist of rain were appropriate for the day, which was dreary and depressing.

His voice dripped compassion as he asked, "Are you sure you can drive? Why not come back inside until you've calmed down a bit?"

She whipped around, her green eyes flashing. "I will never step foot in that house again. Your friend Matt is a jerk!"

Braxton nodded. "Yes, he is."

"Well, unlike the rest of you, I can't and won't put up with him. Jonathan made it clear today how he really feels about me."

"Patience!" Jonathan yelled, but she ignored him.

She hugged Braxton for the last time and climbed into the car. She paused for a moment to collect her thoughts. She wondered if she was strong enough to drive away. As mad as she felt, there remained a part of her that wanted to return to him, to give him a chance to explain. Glancing over her shoulder, she noticed that Braxton had gone inside, but Jonathan remained on the grass a few feet away with his head down. She drew in a sharp breath, turning the ignition with a trembling hand. No, nothing he said could change the fact that he hadn't stood up for her. And there was no telling what else went on behind her back. She put the car in drive, bracing herself for the many weeks of mourning that lay ahead.

PART 2:

DAX

Chapter 17

"Happy New Year!" Sister Camden pulled Patience into a huge bear hug, practically squeezing the life out of her. She smiled as she kissed the elderly woman on the cheek, her heart filled with love for the lady who gave so much of herself to the church. Jeannette Camden was one of those rare individuals who did not have a mean bone in her body. She and her husband Carl were *always* at church. He was a deacon, and she was the head of the Mission and Social Action Committee, among other things. Patience always felt guilty around her, thinking she needed to join the choir or attend prayer meetings after hanging out with her. If there were different levels in Heaven, she knew Jeannette would be on a much higher one than her when they passed on.

"Happy New Year to you, too!" she responded, toying with the bracelet her mother had given her. She wore a simple yet elegant black dress and heels, and her curls were piled high on her head, held in place with a hairclip. She hadn't applied makeup, so she could have passed for seventeen, and her skin was pale from lack of sun. She'd lost some weight since the breakup with Jonathan, so her already-thin frame appeared even smaller. The sparkle in her eyes was gone, and no matter how much she smiled, one could sense the sadness lurking beneath.

Patience was glad she had changed her mind, deciding at the last minute to attend the church's New Year Celebration. She'd been so down in the dumps during the Christmas break, and it took everything she had to push through the depression and get out of the house. She compared the feeling to grieving the loss of a loved one, although it wasn't as serious as death, of course. However, the morning after the blowup at Jonathan's, she'd woken up *feeling* as if a part of her had died, yet she didn't dare tell anyone. After all, to outsiders, her relationship with him had been brief and couldn't possibly have left her as bereft as she was. Even so, the intensity of their romance led her to believe she could have fallen in love with him. Saying good bye to him had cut through her like a knife.

"Are your parents here, sweetie?"

"Yes, they're making their rounds with Cole." She stood on her tiptoes and found them standing at the far end of the room, kissing and embracing everyone within reach. Although Cole attended a different church, he was a frequent visitor to New Mount Zion, Patience's home church. And everyone loved him, always welcoming him with open arms.

Sister Camden took hold of her hand, pressing an envelope into it with a smile. "Here's a little something for all your hard work this month." The envelope wasn't sealed, and Patience could see the one-hundred-dollar bill sticking halfway out.

She shook her head. "No, I couldn't . . ."

"Don't be absurd! You helped us so much with the holiday fair, and Sister Jackson said she didn't know how she would have made it without you." Margaret Jackson was the director of the children's church.

"With the flu going around, many of the teachers were out, and she was in a terrible bind. Yet there you were, an angel who came to the rescue."

"It was my pleasure. I love the kids and enjoyed every minute of it."

The older woman grinned. "I know. Everyone could see how good you were with the little ones. And they adore you. You're such a joy to be around!"

Patience smiled. "Thank you. Anytime you need help, feel free to ask."

Jeannette winked. "Honey, don't tell me that! We'll use you up!"

"I like being used!"

The two laughed, and Jeannette hugged her once more before catching sight of her husband at the buffet table. She narrowed her dark brown eyes. "Aha! There's Carl with a huge cookie in one hand and a brownie in the other. We're supposed to be on a diet. He's in big trouble!"

"Watching your weight during the holidays seems torturous to me."

Jeannette winked. "Don't let Carl hear you say that." Setting her sights on Mr. Camden, she walked away quickly. Patience giggled when Carl saw his wife storming toward him and tried hiding the desserts under a napkin. They were a cute couple, loved and respected by their church family.

Seeing the yummy-looking treats made her realize she needed something sweet to eat. Making her way through the crowd, she smiled and waved at the children she had taken care

165

of in the children's ministry. A family she'd babysat for years ago stopped her to chat, as well. And one of the teenagers from the choir pulled her aside to ask how her Christmas was, blushing profusely and gazing down at the floor between sentences, his hands dug deep in the pockets of his trousers. Everyone knew he had a crush on her and thought it was adorable. She talked to him for a while, trying to ease the awkwardness she knew he felt.

By the time she reached the table, she was famished. She poured herself a cup of punch and then reached for a paper plate to hold her Rice Krispies treats. It was the first time she'd actually craved food in two weeks, which was a miracle. She briefly wondered if she should go find Cole. Standing near the table, she decided to stay put, especially since she was holding a Styrofoam cup with red punch inside. As clumsy as she was, she didn't need to walk around while eating. She took a sip of the sugary beverage, turning to watch the crowd on her right, when she bumped into someone who was passing by. He whipped around to face her, and she could see that the red juice had splashed all over the front of his white, button-down shirt.

"Oh my gosh! I am so, so sorry," Patience uttered, mentally kicking herself for drinking something red in the first place. She grabbed a bunch of napkins and began blotting his shirt with them.

The young man smiled. "Don't worry about it."

"Ok, it's finally dawning on me that these napkins aren't helping the situation. The ugly red stain is here to stay."

He laughed good-naturedly.

"I am really very sorry," she repeated, almost too embarrassed to notice how gorgeous he was.

"It's not a problem at all. Please stop apologizing."

She blushed. "I'm like a child and either need to drink only clear beverages or carry them around in a sippy cup!"

He chuckled. "There's nothing wrong with that! I should wear a bib whenever I eat ... anything!"

She walked over to the trash can to get rid of the weapon, pausing for a moment to glance back at him. He was watching her with interest, and it was then that she realized just how beautiful he was. He appeared to be five foot ten or so, with a slim build and short, spiky blond hair. His blue eyes were dark, almost violet in color, and his tanned skin looked great against the white shirt with the red stain in front. She just knew he was a model or actor. No one could be that stunning and not be on television.

Patience watched as one of the ministers approached the young man to chat, so she seized the opportunity to disappear. She was too self-conscious to be in his presence after ruining his shirt. *He must think I'm a moron*, she thought as she covered her face with one hand. *I wonder if there's a support group for klutzes.* She scanned the crowd for her parents, spotting them near the coatrack up front. Figuring they were getting ready to leave, she began weaving through the guests once again, pausing every few steps to say good bye to someone.

"Sister McKlendon, it was so good to see you tonight!" Brother Harris kissed her cheek tenderly.

"Patience, I hope the New Year brings you many blessings!" Brother Smith hugged her warmly.

She finally made it to her parents, and Cole met them outside a few minutes later. It was freezing, and he helped her button her jacket.

"Thanks, Dad," she joked as he stood an inch away from her, frowning while he concentrated on keeping her warm.

"No problem, pumpkin," he replied, and they burst into laughter. Although she gave him a hard time, she secretly loved the way he protected her like a big brother would. He was always ready to fight anyone who messed with her, and if she was sick, he was the first one at her bedside with chicken soup. In a way, he loved her more than anyone, minus Sharise and John, of course. She knew he would do anything to keep her from harm.

Still standing in front of her, he smiled. "Who was that ugly guy you spilled juice on earlier?"

"You saw that?"

"Yep, and I know you were devastated."

She shivered. "I don't know his name. I've never seen him here before."

"Yeah, I saw him hanging out with a couple of guys who are members here. Maybe he was just visiting. Now come on, let's get you out of this cold, night air." Cole took her by the hand, and they ran to catch up with her parents, who were already in the car.

Chapter 18

January didn't start off as depressing as Patience had thought it would. With another week of vacation ahead of her, she'd figured having that much spare time to ruminate about Jonathan would be tough. Yet she had an exceptional support system. Her family and friends really came through, each one determined to distract her. On Monday, she went to the movies with Jana, and then they returned to Jana's place to pamper themselves, painting each other's toenails and meditating to classical music. Patience whipped up a facial mask made of oatmeal, honey, and yogurt, insisting it was great for dry skin. Later that evening, Jana's new boyfriend came over to cook for them.

She spent Tuesday and Wednesday with her parents, and Cole was sweet enough to invite her to his boys' night out with Jarrod and Cary on Thursday. His friends liked her a lot, so it took absolutely no bribing on his part for them to include her. And Friday, he took her ice-skating, which was a blast for them both. They resembled two children frolicking around, pushing each other down and attempting risky moves only professional skaters should. Cole was pretty athletic, yet he fell more times than she could count. Her clumsiness was taken up a notch on the ice, which wasn't a surprise to either of them. At one point, she picked up speed and fell into a good rhythm only to realize, as she headed toward the wall, that she couldn't turn in time. She ran into the wall at full force, collapsing on the ice with a *thud*. Cole was at her side in a millisecond, stooping to bring her back to a standing position.

"Ouch! That hurt so bad I can't be embarrassed. My right hip will be bruised tomorrow, I'm sure of it."

He grabbed her gloved hand. "You don't have hips. Now, let's get some hot chocolate and rest for a while."

Before Patience knew it, Saturday morning was upon her. She had no plans other than to help with childcare again at New Mount Zion. Sister Jackson had called her the night before, frantic, explaining that one of the members was getting married and she was in desperate need of assistance. Ten children were on the list to be there, but she only had two caregivers. The wedding was scheduled for four p.m., and Margaret wondered if she could be there by three.

"Of course! I'm more than happy to help," Patience assured. The week had gone so well, and she wanted to keep up the momentum. She was in high spirits as she pulled her Honda into the church's parking lot. Dressed in a powder-blue sweater, jeans, and sneakers, she entered the building with a huge grin. There was something about being in the house of the Lord, among others who loved and worshipped Him, that always comforted her. She knew bad things could happen in the church just like everywhere else, but she still felt protected there. Everyone was so inviting and earnest.

"Sister McKlendon!" Margaret Jackson came running toward her, the high heels she wore making *clickety-clack* sounds that echoed in the hallway. "I've never been so happy to see anyone in my life! Come to me, my sweet child!"

Patience laughed, welcoming the director's warm embrace.

"Thank you so much for helping us out today. Just between you and me, I don't understand why the bride-to-be told the guests that childcare would be provided. Don't these people have babysitters?" She continued to rant while leading Patience to the Terrific Threes room. As they opened the door, she caught sight of a small boy jumping off of one of the tables and into a huge container of stuffed animals. The two women exchanged a horrified look.

"At least he had a soft landing," Patience said with a wink.

They watched as another child took a huge bite of a crayon, exclaiming, "Yummy!" to her friend. On the opposite side of the room, two others were crying and whining their parents' names, while the boy who loved to jump decided to climb onto an even higher cabinet, preparing for his next big stunt. Another girl was running with scissors, screaming at the top of her lungs. And a curly-haired boy stood in front of the window with scissors of his own, getting ready to cut the mini-blind cord. The teenager who was supervising ran over to him, trying her best to regain control of the energetic children.

Sister Jackson stepped in quickly. "Carter, get down this instant!" she commanded to the climber with a stern look.

"Okay," Carter shouted gleefully, his tiny body sailing expertly through the air. He landed with a *thud* on his feet, unharmed.

After scolding him, Margaret introduced Patience to Sara, the frazzled young helper.

"Boy, am I glad to meet you!" Sara said, shaking her hand

and glancing around with wide eyes. "As you can see, I have no control in here."

Patience hung her jacket and purse on the coat rack and then walked to the center of the room. Out of the corner of her eye, she noticed the guy she'd spilled red punch on the week before standing in the doorway.

"Well, with Jesus' help, we can regain control," she continued, clapping her hands to get the kids' attention. Sister Jackson and Sara laughed, and the young man raised an eyebrow with interest, leaning against the wall with his hands in his pockets.

"Okay, I want everyone to come and sit in a circle on the floor ... over here ... Carter, get down!" She motioned for the two weeping girls to join them. As soon as everyone was seated, she sat between Carter and the crayon-eater. She didn't feel like making any trips to the ER, nor did she want to perform the Heimlich.

"Let's go around the circle and tell what we got for Christmas."

Sister Jackson whispered, "I guess it's safe to leave now." She winked and tiptoed out of the room. The young man grinned, approaching the group tentatively. Standing above Patience, he said,

"Sister Camden told me I was needed here. She said something about wild, uncontrollable three-year-olds taking over the church." He chuckled.

"We *are* wild!" Carter confessed proudly, and the others snickered.

"My mommy told me I have ADP," the boy who'd had the scissors earlier piped in.

"You mean ADD," Patience corrected with a smile.

"Uh-huh." He wiped his runny nose with his shirtsleeve, so Sara went to find a Kleenex. Mr. Mysterious squatted next to the children, extending a hand to Patience.

"By the way, my name is Dax. Dax Christian."

He flashed a killer smile, causing even the children to pause and stare, openmouthed, at the beautiful man. He wore black slacks with a navy shirt that made his eyes appear more blue than purple, as they had on New Year's Eve. Everyone sat temporarily hypnotized by his looks alone. But the thing that made him more appealing was his friendly personality. Patience felt her mouth hanging open, positive she was drooling. For a moment, she couldn't find her voice.

It was Sara who finally broke the silence.

"You're here to help us? That's great!"

He shrugged. "Sure, if you need me."

"We need you," Patience and Sara blurted out in unison. The kids giggled.

He grinned, and again, they all froze briefly. Patience wondered if he modeled for *GQ*.

"Seems to me the kids are behaving now," he observed.

One of the girls who'd been weeping spoke up. "I'm gonna cry again in a minute."

Dax went over to her, sitting down with his legs crossed like the others.

"If you *know* you're going to cry, maybe we can prevent it. I bet you'll be happy when you tell me what Santa brought you." He winked at Patience, and she blushed.

"He gave me a new puppy! He bites all the time, and it

173

hurts. He's my new bestest friend," the child gushed, her pretty brown face lighting up before everyone's eyes.

Dax smiled. "What's his name?"

"Puppy."

The children snickered.

"I love that name," Patience commented, taking a marker away from the crayon-eater. Apparently she had a bunch of knickknacks stashed in her pockets. "What are you going to call him when he grows into a dog?"

"Doggie."

Patience nodded. "Oh, I see."

"I got a baby sister," Carter yelled.

"Aww, what's her name?" Sara asked.

"I don't remember. I wanted a brother anyway."

After making it around the circle, the children were separated into groups. Patience read stories to Carter, Stella- the eater of dangerous objects, and two others. Sara played games with the weepy girls, and Dax assisted the other two boys and girl with an art project. Lastly, one boy sat playing with Legos in the corner. Then, the caregivers rotated the groups, so that everyone had a chance to do everything. More important, no one had time to be mischievous.

At four fifteen, they served a snack. The kids were calm and behaving pretty well. Patience grabbed a handful of Chex Mix as she chatted with Sara and Dax. They were sitting with the children, thankful to have a tiny break from activities.

Tucking a curl behind her ear, she grinned at Stella. "Now doesn't this taste better than crayons?"

Stella nodded. "Uh-huh, especially the M&Ms."

Dax chuckled. "I used to eat dirt when I was little."

"That sounds good," the curly-haired boy said.

Stella appeared to be lost in thought for a second and then added, "My sister eats bugs."

"She does? How old is she?" Patience asked.

"Three."

Patience raised an eyebrow. "You're three as well, correct?"

"Correct. Lyla's my twin sister."

"Why isn't she here with you?"

Stella took a sip of her juice. "She has a cold. Daddy stayed home with her."

Patience leaned forward, resting her elbows on the table as she listened. Twins were fascinating to her. "Does Lyla look like you?"

"No, her hair is dark." She began twirling her long, blonde hair absentmindedly. "I'm prettier, too."

The entire group burst into laughter, and Stella shrugged. "Well, I am."

* * *

Patience headed to her car, shivering as she searched for her keys in the well-lit parking lot. The afternoon had flown by, thanks to the rambunctious children and steady excitement Carter had provided. After snack, the caregivers had bundled the kids up and taken them on the playground to release their pent-up energy. The sad girls had perked up, distracted by the fun activities, and the only partial emergency they'd experienced was when the curly-haired boy had stuck a small rock in Stella's ear. Blessedly, Dax was able to retrieve it, and the child had been so brave. She had stood perfectly still as he recovered the rock with the tweezers Sara supplied. They were relieved beyond words to have avoided a trip to the ER.

Unable to find her keys, she turned and began retracing her steps to the building. It was then that she spotted Dax sprinting toward her, keys dangling from his hand.

"I'm afraid you won't get far without these," he said, panting slightly. "And I just discovered I'm out of shape! Whew, I need to catch my breath!"

She giggled. "Don't be so hard on yourself. It's a long way from the Terrific Threes classroom!"

He appeared unconvinced. "That's sweet of you to say, but it's so untrue."

Handing her the keys, he cocked his head to the side. "You probably never become short-winded. Looks like you work out regularly."

She knew her face was crimson red. Her cheeks felt as if they were on fire. She averted her eyes, focusing on the wedding guests leaving the church.

He touched her shoulder, his smile replaced with a frown. "I'm sorry. I didn't mean to make you uncomfortable."

Patience shifted her weight from one foot to the other. "It's okay. I'm not good at accepting compliments."

Dax took a step closer, his gaze never wavering from hers.

"I would think that someone with your undeniable beauty would be used to praise from others."

Again, she felt her face burning, but this time she just thanked him.

"*Do you* work out?" he asked, and she caught a whiff of his cologne.

"Every now and then I jog . . ."

He grinned from ear to ear. "We should go jogging some-time!"

"You like to run?"

He smirked. "Not particularly, but I can endure it to spend time with you."

"I haven't seen you here before last week. Did you just join the church?" she asked, attempting to change the subject.

"No, my buddy's a member. You may know him. His name is Will McAllister."

She nodded. "Yes, I do! His dad is a deacon, and his sister teaches Sunday school for my age group. I've gone a couple of times. They're a nice family."

"They *are*. Will's been inviting me to visit for the last five months, so I decided it was time."

"How long have you known him?"

"Five months," he laughed.

"Well, I'm glad you relented. This is a delightful church."

Patience and Dax chatted a few more minutes before they were interrupted by her ringing cell. She didn't bother answer-ing it, certain it was just her mother or Jana checking up on her. However, she realized she couldn't stand there gazing at this beautiful man all night. The once-busy parking lot was nearly empty; only the janitor hurried inside the building, while a cou-ple of teens ran to their cars, anxious to escape the cold.

As if reading her mind, he grinned. "I guess I better let you get home now."

She smiled. "Okay, I had fun working with you today."

"Likewise. You were so good with the children. Are you coming to church tomorrow?"

She opened the car door, pausing a moment to look into his purplish-blue eyes. "Yes."

"Great! Then I'll see you in the morning."

Chapter 19

Dax found Patience sitting in the last pew and quietly slid next to her with a smile. The choir was singing "Amazing Grace," a song that always brought her close to tears. She asked God for grace and mercy, and knew He helped her to show more grace to others. He was her source of strength, and she always found peace when seeking Him. The lyrics reminded her of His forgiveness, which usually made her weepy. She just couldn't wrap her mind around the fact that He loved her so much.

"You okay?" Dax whispered as one of the ushers handed her a tissue.

"Yes, I'm fine. Sometimes I get emotional in church. I feel so . . . unworthy, ya know?"

"I understand exactly what you mean. I'm surprised they don't lock the doors when they see me approaching."

She giggled. "You're crazy."

The choir sang one more song, and then the preacher took his place behind the podium, opening with a prayer. Despite her efforts, Patience's mind began to wander. She was excited that Dax had shown up that morning. And of course, he looked even more spectacular than the night before. She tried not to be a shallow person, but she just couldn't help it. He was absolutely the most gorgeous person she'd seen in a while. Immediately, guilt swept over her, for she was in church, after all. And besides, as of a week ago, she had sworn off men. Dating was too difficult.

Ironically, the sermon was on pressing forward in times of trouble and trying not to be discouraged. Both she and Dax enjoyed the service, and afterward, they mingled with everyone. They spotted Will and his sister helping set up for the pastor's anniversary dinner that was scheduled for later that evening. It seemed the church always had something going on, a wedding or revival or baptism. New Mount Zion was huge, and the building was gorgeous, which made it the number-one choice for events to be held there.

About an hour later, Patience and Dax said their good-byes to everyone and headed outside. They squinted as their eyes adjusted to the bright sunlight, a welcome surprise after all the dreary days they'd endured. The two slowly made their way to her car, each lost in thought. She wondered what his plans were for the rest of the day. She had no idea what lay ahead for her. Part of her wanted to hang out at home with Rory and work on her novel. Yet the other part needed to be around people, or at least *one* person, so she didn't have to be alone with her thoughts. After a breakup, she was prone to sinking into an abyss of negativity and self-doubt. Besides, the day was too pretty to be locked up indoors.

He shoved his hands in his pants pockets as the two stood facing each other awkwardly.

After what seemed an eternity, she sighed.

"Um, it was great sitting by you at church." As soon as the

words escaped her mouth, she wanted to gag. She sounded so corny.

He laughed. "I'm glad. I rather enjoyed sitting next to you, as well." Taking a step closer, he reached up to tuck a curl behind her ear. Instantly, she felt as if a spark of electricity shot through her.

He quickly withdrew his hand, his eyes open as wide as if he'd seen a ghost. "Did you feel that?"

"What?" She didn't know if he meant the same thing she was thinking.

Pausing a moment, Dax took a step backward. He ran a hand through his hair. "Never mind," he mumbled.

Patience let it go. She didn't want to acknowledge the fact that something weird had happened. Of course she'd felt the electrical current when he had touched her. But that wasn't something she wanted to get into right now.

Instead, she shrugged. "I guess I better go."

"What do you have planned for today?"

"So far I don't have anything going on. What about you?"

"I may have a date," he said softly.

Her heart sank. Of course he dated! From what she knew about him so far, he had many characteristics any woman would be attracted to. He exuded friendliness and warmth, liked kids, had a gorgeous face and body, and appeared intelligent. She couldn't imagine him single, unless he went out with many different women. And yet . . . he didn't strike her as the player type. She shook her head, giggling suddenly. Here she was, trying to figure him out, and he had plans to go on a date with someone. She was ridiculous sometimes.

"Oh, well, I need to let you go, then," she said with a giggle.

181

"*What* is so funny?"

"I'm laughing at myself ... never mind ... have a great week," she said, stumbling over her words. She was so embarrassed, ready to make a fast escape before she said something else stupid.

Dax smiled broadly. "You are so cute."

"I am?"

"Would you like to go out with me today?"

Her heart rate accelerated. He had been talking about her.

"Sure."

* * *

"We'll start with the grilled artichoke and spinach dip," Dax told the waitress at Fireside Pies, a Dallas restaurant known for its incredibly delicious pizza and pasta. They sat on the patio, which had an outdoor fireplace ringed with ironwork and, in the summer, was surrounded by mixed greenery that beckoned for people to eat outside. Patience loved the outdoors and was grateful the weather wasn't too hot or cold. She inhaled deeply, feeling refreshed and happy.

"Would you like a moment to look over the menus while I get your appetizer?"

Dax glanced at Patience, who winked.

"Nah, that's okay. We'll have the Burrata Mozzarella Pie, please," he replied.

The waitress walked away, and Patience looked around with interest. The place was busy for a Sunday afternoon. She guessed a lot of people had cabin fever, choosing this restaurant for its beautiful scenery and tasty food. Many were dressed up, probably coming straight from church. She and Cole had eaten here numerous times before, and the crowd was usually young and eclectic, especially on Saturday nights. And Fireside Pies' staff was always friendly and upbeat. She loved it.

"You're beautiful," Dax said suddenly, and she turned her attention back to him, startled.

"Really?" she replied, and then her face burned with embarrassment. So far, her responses to his compliments had been less than gracious.

"Yes, really!" He chuckled, leaning forward to rest his elbows on the table and gaze at her.

"Patience, you crack me up!" Shaking his head, he took a sip of water.

"I do seem to make you laugh quite often," she said, playing with her napkin absentmindedly. It was odd, but she felt both comfortable and nervous around him, and she didn't know how to handle it. His eyes bore right through her, she was sure of it, as if he could see her soul. She felt naked, exposed ... and it wouldn't have surprised her if he had the power to read her mind.

"You have no idea how endearing you are."

The two jumped at the sound of a high-pitched scream from a child nearby. They turned to see the little boy throw himself on the floor, his mother watching in dismay and the father reaching down to scoop him up. Patience smiled. The child couldn't have been more than two years of age, and Dax grinned.

"Toddlers- you gotta love them."

Their waitress returned with the chips and spinach dip, her eyes dancing with laughter. She had overheard Dax. "Yes, that family comes here once a week, and no one wants to wait on them. That kid throws a tantrum every time, and the parents always give in."

Patience shook her head. "I feel sorry for them. How embarrassing!"

The server rolled her eyes. "Well, *I* don't! They created that monster, so now they have to deal with him." She paused. "Can I get you anything else?"

"No, thanks, we're good," Dax answered. When the waitress was out of earshot, he shrugged. "My parents wouldn't have tolerated tizzies. If I even thought about acting crazy as a child, all my dad had to do was give me a certain look, and I'd shape up." Taking a chip and scooping it into the dip, he added, "And if he wasn't there to glare at me, my mom was!"

Wondering if she should act like a lady and take a tiny bite of food, she reached for a chip and then decided to be herself. Grabbing her spoon, she dug it into the dip and spread a huge glob onto her chip, biting into it with satisfaction. She wasn't like other girls who were too shy to eat in front of their dates. Besides, she loved artichoke and spinach. And she was hungry.

"Your parents were strict, huh?" she responded between bites.

"Yes."

"Are you close to them?"

"No."

Patience dabbed her mouth with a napkin. "Were you guys ever close?" she asked, her brows furrowed.

"No."

"Do you have any siblings?"

"No."

184

Sitting back in her chair, it was her turn to study him. Although he had been the one to bring up the subject of his family, his posture and facial expression told her the topic was now closed. His dark blue eyes were focused on the tablecloth, and his shoulders were hunched.

Leaning forward, she reached over and gently cupped his chin with her hand, and he looked at her. "Are you okay?"

He smiled. "Sure, I'm fine."

The waitress came with their entrée, so Patience seized the opportunity to change the subject. "I love this stuff! Coley and I order it every time we come."

Dax picked up the knife to cut her a slice of the heavenly pizza. "I agree! I've been here with Will. While he always tries something different, I stick with this."

As they ate, the two chatted like old friends. He had a great sense of humor and told her funny stories about his best friend and some of his cousins, whom he considered friends. They were his aunt's two children, on his mom's side of the family.

"Yeah, Blake and Shelton are like the brothers I never had. We're close in age so-"

"Which is . . . ?" she interrupted.

"Oh, I'm twenty-five."

Perfect, she thought to herself. "Do they live here?"

He nodded. "Yep, they're in Carrollton, so I see them all the time."

"That's cool," she said, delighted to see him perk up at the mention of his cousins.

"What about you? Are you close to your family?"

"My parents are my best friends," she admitted, and then

185

she felt a stab of guilt. She didn't want to rub their wonderful relationship in his face.

"Aww, that's sweet. Do you have any siblings?"

Patience took a long drink, stalling. Finally, she shook her head no and then asked what he did for a living.

"I'm a copy editor for *Dallas Magazine*. Do you like being an only child?"

"Dax, I think we should talk about other things besides my family."

He appeared confused. "Why?"

She brushed a lock of hair off her shoulder. "Well, because you didn't seem too happy with that topic of conversation earlier ..."

He waved a hand dismissively. "I just don't want to discuss *my* parents!"

They both laughed.

He reached across the table to place his hand on top of hers, and again, she felt the spark, the tiny shock she'd experienced earlier at the church. And from the expression on his face, she could tell he felt it, too. But this time, he didn't jerk his hand away.

"I want to know everything about you," he said softly. They were in their own little world amid the hustle and bustle of the busy restaurant.

"Are you sure? We resemble *Leave it to Beaver*. It's sickening, at best," she warned.

"Tell me everything."

Chapter 20

Dax walked Patience to her door, his hands casually tucked into his pants pockets. It was only four o'clock, but the sun was hiding behind the clouds, making it appear later. She glanced sideways at her new friend, a smile tugging at her lips. She'd had a great time with him and hoped he felt the same. She didn't want him to leave just yet, for she didn't know when she would see him again. It was dramatic for her to think that way, but it couldn't be helped.

The two faced each other on the porch as Rory began barking and throwing his body against the door.

Dax laughed. "Whoa, I guess you have a pet! Is it a dog or a wolf?"

Patience put the key in the lock. "His bark is worse than his bite. Actually, he doesn't bite. Rory's harmless." She paused. "Are you afraid of dogs?"

"I'm only scared of cats, so we're good."

She smiled. "Me, too! Wow, you're the first person I've met with the same fear! Most people laugh when they find out." She opened the door, and Rory burst out, immediately jumping up on Dax like a wild animal.

"Rory, get down! I am so sorry," she apologized as she put her dog in a gentle headlock.

Dax knelt down to pat him. "Don't worry about it. He's adorable. Hey, Rory! What's up, buddy?"

Patience hesitated. She wanted to invite him in but didn't want him to feel obligated to stay. Besides, she didn't know why she had gone to lunch with him in the first place. This was way too soon to be entertaining men, in her eyes. The mourning period for Jonathan hadn't ended, and it was disrespectful and unhealthy to have a crush on someone new. She tilted her head to the side, watching in amusement as Dax picked up a stick lying nearby and began playing fetch with Rory. They obviously hit it off and were becoming fast friends.

She sat on the step and daydreamed while the two continued to play, not wanting to interrupt their bonding time. Suddenly she felt her cell vibrate in her purse.

"Hello?"

"Hi, it's Jonathan."

She sat up straighter, her mouth suddenly dry. She couldn't believe he had the nerve to call her. For a moment, words escaped her. Everything around her seemed to fade as she focused on him.

"Did I lose you?" he asked, his voice deep and incredibly sexy.

Shaking her head, she finally spoke. "No, I'm here."

"What are you doing?"

Her eyes flew to Dax, who was now running up and down the sidewalk with Rory chasing him. She wondered how he had that much energy after eating a big meal.

"I'm sitting outside. What's up?"

"Is it okay if I come over tonight? I want to talk to you."

But Patience shook her head. "I don't think that's a bright idea. Let's just move on."

"Please . . ." he began, but she cut him off, her words shaky.

"Jonathan, don't make this harder. I can't do this." To her dismay, her eyes began to well up, and Dax was headed her way. "I have to go," she whispered sadly, a variety of emotions residing inside her. She felt torn, wanting to both kiss and strangle her ex-boyfriend at the same time.

Dax sat next to her, his brows knit in concern as he watched her. Unable to calm down, Rory continued running laps around the yard.

"Can I call you later, then?" Jonathan persisted.

"I'll be busy."

"Please don't give up on me," he pleaded. "I will let you go for now, but you can expect to hear from me soon. Patience, I have something to tell you. Just give me one more chance, baby!"

She stared at her phone for a second after he'd hung up, unsure of what to do. The devil on her shoulder told her to invite him over and patch things up, opening herself up to more heartache. The angel on her other shoulder said to be gentle yet firm, severing ties with him so she could finally begin to heal. She ached for him, though, especially after hearing his voice.

Dax nudged her with his elbow. "This is the second time I've seen you cry. And I just met you last week!"

"I'm not crying."

"Hmm. Okay. So, you're happy right now?"

Blinking away the tears, she hopped up, brushing the dust off her dress. She held a hand out to help him up. Squaring her shoulders, she smiled broadly. "Would you like to come in for a while?"

He let out a sigh, his purplish-blue eyes lighting up instantly. "I thought you'd never ask."

* * *

"So, what exactly does a copy editor do?" It was ten p.m., and Patience was dressed for bed, her cell cradled between her ear and shoulder. Dax had stayed over until almost nine and then promised to call her when he made it home. He had, and they'd been on the phone ever since. She was so glad she'd invited him in earlier. They'd watched a movie and talked, having fun getting to know each other better.

"Well, I look for errors in articles, and I make sure the piece says what it means and means what it says."

She laughed. "Ah, so you do more than just fix punctuation mistakes!"

"Absolutely! My job includes what some call the five Cs. I have to ensure that the article is clear, correct, concise, comprehensible, and consistent."

She slid her feet out of the fuzzy slippers her dad had given her for Christmas. "Well, don't you sound smart? I may have to hire you to edit *my* novel."

"You wrote a book? What's the title?"

"I'm not sure yet. I may call it *Which One?*"

"What's the premise?"

Patience shooed Rory off her bed so she could pull the comforter back, pausing for a second to think. "The main character is a white male dating two women. One is African-American and the other, Caucasian. He's forced to choose between them when they find out about each other. It would be easier for him to stay with the white one, for obvious reasons. But he's torn because his feelings for both run deep."

Dax whistled. "The plot sounds interesting and pretty unique. Okay, I'll edit for free."

She grinned. He always seemed to make her smile. "That's an offer even I can afford. I'll take it!"

After a brief silence, he said, "On second thought, proofreading can be a ton of work, with lots of time involved, and it *is* hard on the eyes. I better charge ya." She could almost see his wicked grin through her phone.

Burying herself deeper under the covers, she closed her eyes contentedly. "Name your price."

"You have to go on a second date with me."

Her green eyes popped open. "Excuse me, but when did we go on our first one?"

"Um, today?" he answered, sounding perplexed. "Do you have an identical twin pretending to be you? I swear I went out with this beautiful, intriguing, and really sweet woman today-"

"Oh, that was me," she interrupted, flattered by his words, "but that wasn't a date. I'm sorry."

He sighed. "Wow, it's a good thing I have high self-esteem. Otherwise, I'd be crushed."

"I'm so sorry! I just got out of a relationship. I've given up on dating."

"You're too cute to even think something like that."

Patience sat up in the bed, her curly hair a tangled mess around her. "Thank you. I do have faults, you know."

"It's a waste of time to try talking me out of it. I'm smitten."

191

She couldn't suppress a giggle. "I'm clumsy, too sensitive, and weak-willed."

"You can add to that list a morning person. I don't get along with people who are perky before eleven a.m."

Stifling a yawn, she decided to let it go for now. His mind was made up. He had a crush on her.

"I can't wait until next weekend," he told her.

"What's happening then?"

"We're going on our first date."

Chapter 21

Staying true to his word, Dax called Patience on Wednesday evening to make plans for Friday night. Against her better judgment, she agreed to dinner and a movie. However, she reiterated beforehand that their outing wouldn't be a date. They were simply friends with nothing better to do than hang out with each other. Yet, when she opened the door on Friday, she became nervous. He stood on the porch holding a bouquet of white roses, a wide smile on his perfectly chiseled face. Dressed casual in jeans and a long-sleeved black turtleneck, she decided then and there that he could wear a trash bag and be gorgeous.

She held Rory's collar as Dax stepped inside. He handed her the roses, his eyes traveling over her approvingly.

"You're stunning," he said softly.

She accepted the flowers, her own eyes downcast. "Thanks. I thought we said this wasn't a date."

"*You* said it, not me."

"Dax," she began, but he took a step closer, almost stepping on Rory in the process. Putting a finger on her lips, he turned serious in the dimly lit foyer.

"Shh," he whispered, his face just an inch away, his minty breath tickling her nose. "It doesn't matter what we call it.

The fact is I like you and want to get to know you better." He shrugged. "If you need to put a wall up to protect yourself because you've been hurt, it's okay. I understand."

She stood motionless, barely breathing while digesting his words.

"Patience, I know this is forward, but I'm just being honest. As we get closer, you'll find that I'm a very direct person. I don't believe in playing games or beating around the bush. I am extremely attracted to you physically and on a deeper level, too. Ever since you spilled juice all over me, I haven't been able to get you off of my mind."

Rory sat by their feet, sniffing the flowers and then sneezing.

She sighed. "I don't know what to say."

He took a step backward, and she could tell he was disappointed. "There's no need to respond. You've been up front with me, and I appreciate that. We can take things slowly. Now, go put those flowers in some water so we can go. I can't wait to see this movie."

She headed toward the kitchen. "Which one are we seeing?" On Wednesday they had agreed on him picking the movie and she could choose the restaurant.

"*Death is Waiting*."

* * *

"You're as pale as a ghost. I'm slightly worried." Dax held the car door open, and Patience slid inside.

"Yes, but I'll be all right," she lied through clenched teeth. She waited for him to walk around to his side of the vehicle, wondering what she would do if some zombie snatched him before he made it in. It didn't help that the theater parking lot had very little lighting, nor was it comforting that he would have to take her home at some point, leaving her all alone to protect herself. The fact that she had Rory left her even more frightened. He was too friendly to be of any help if a monster broke into her home.

He started the ignition, turning the heater on full blast as he watched her. "I apologize. I don't remember you telling me about your fear of horror flicks."

"I probably didn't. It's no big deal. I'm fine." She immediately thought of the night she and Jonathan had double-dated with Matt and Tricia. The guys had chosen a scary movie, as well. That seemed to be the popular genre at the moment.

He reached over, gently taking her hand in his. "I promise we'll see *Annie* next time," he reassured, which made her burst out laughing.

"Come on! I can't appear that pathetic to you!"

"On the contrary, you seem like a sweet, vulnerable young woman. It's refreshing, actually. Most girls act so tough, bristling if I open a door for them. You're not like that. You wear your heart on your sleeve and have a very caring nature."

They sat in silence for a while, cozy in his warm car. She had no idea how to respond to all of his praises. She was afraid to admit, even to herself, that she liked him so much more each time they were together. His charm and no-nonsense attitude hooked her, but she had to be careful. She couldn't jump into a rebound romance.

"What are you thinking?" he asked, his voice husky.

"I'm wondering how many girls you take out per week and tell these things to," she teased, knowing he wasn't the type.

He clutched his chest, feigning surprise. "I cannot believe you just said that. I'm hurt, Patience."

She shrugged. "Well, one can't be sure. I mean, look at you! I'm positive women are tripping over one another to beat on your door."

Leaning in closer, he smiled shyly. "The only one I'm opening the door for is you."

She drew in a sharp breath, amazed at the effect he had on her. He was such a smooth talker, but not in a cocky, Don Juan way. It was more of a schoolboy-who-has-a-crush sort of way.

Slowly, he bent his head toward her, and she closed her eyes expectantly. She couldn't believe he was going to kiss her. They'd only known each other two weeks. This wasn't right. It was too soon. Things were moving way too fast. She should pull back before anything drastic happened.

His lips were feathery soft as he kissed ... the tip of her nose.

Her heart sank while relief swept over her. She would have bet money that he was aiming for her mouth. How foolish of her. Exhaling loudly, she opened her eyes and leaned back against the seat.

"I think we should head to the restaurant now," he said as he fastened the seat belt quickly.

* * *

"I had fun tonight." Patience extended a hand to Dax, trying her best to keep it casual. They heard Rory barking inside, and the two faced each other, with Patience planning a fast exit. They had kept the conversation light and upbeat at the seafood place and again in his car on the way to her house. She didn't want to make the mistake of misinterpreting his signals anymore.

"Me, too," he replied hesitantly. Ever since the peck on the nose, he'd been slightly distant, friendly yet reserved. But she didn't attempt to figure him out. She stank at reading body language and facial expressions. He shook her hand, the usual spark shooting through both of their bodies.

"Well, I guess I'll leave." He walked down the driveway, his hands shoved deep into his pockets.

How awkward can this get? she thought, putting the key into the lock.

"Patience?"

She turned around to find him standing by his car, nervously toying with his keys.

"Yes?"

"I'll call you when I get home."

She rolled her eyes. "I should hope so! I need to make sure zombies didn't kidnap you on the way!"

He chuckled."I'd fight them tooth and nail. Nothing is going to keep me from taking you out again."

Chapter 22

The remainder of the weekend was a blur. Patience rose early on Saturday morning to grade papers and take Rory for a long run at the dog park. Afterward, she met Jana for lunch, and then she hung out with her parents until evening. She lost track of time at around six, panicking as she raced home to shower before her dinner date with Cole. He'd called her that morning to invite her over, promising to cook one of her favorite meals and watch chick flicks.

"*I* don't even like girly movies, Cole," she'd reminded him. "Well, some are okay."

He sighed with relief. "Oh yeah, that's right. Great, then I'll just make homemade enchiladas and rice, and we can rent *Sleepy Hollow*," he'd teased.

"I'll ignore that movie suggestion. What's the occasion for spoiling me?"

"I need a Patience fix. I miss you."

"Aww, same here, Coley."

* * *

Dax had texted her that evening, but Patience had turned off her phone while with Cole. She didn't read the messages until close to midnight, when Cole brought her home. She and her best friend had had a great time hanging out and catching up. It had been just like old times. Before the night was over, they promised each other to do this more often.

Glancing at the phone, she smiled. He had texted her! Her stomach did a little flip as she climbed into bed. She couldn't wait to hear his voice but knew it was too late to call. She turned in, deciding to respond on Sunday.

"How are you?" Patience practically sang into the phone the next morning. She woke up in a fantastic mood after spending quality time with her best friend.

Dax chuckled. "I'm obviously not doing better than you! Why so perky?"

She poured dog food in Rory's bowl, which he turned his nose up at. Lately he'd been getting leftover scraps from her meals, so now he considered himself above Kibbles 'n Bits.

"I'm happy to be alive," she answered, realizing how ridiculous she sounded.

"Ugh! Okay, this is why I run from morning people. You guys are sick!"

"Whenever you're done cutting me down, I want to thank you for the sweet texts you sent."

"You're welcome. You were busy all day?"

She relayed the events to him, and he whistled. "It's a good thing I'm asking you out now, as opposed to yesterday."

Leaning against the kitchen counter, she looked out the window. The sun shone brightly, but the air must have still been cool. One of the kids in the neighborhood zoomed through her yard on his bicycle, wearing a jacket.

"What do you have in mind?" she asked.

"Do you like museums?"

"No."

He laughed. "I've never heard of a teacher who didn't like museums. We could go to the Dallas Aquarium."

"Now that's more like it!"

* * *

Dax held Patience's hand as they walked through the aquarium chatting animatedly about their jobs.

"I love teaching. Not only do I get to educate the youth, I also have the opportunity to wear many hats. I'm a therapist, mother, and nurse. And every day is an adventure."

They stopped in front of the tank with otters, and Dax smiled broadly. "I bet! Teens are quite intimidating to me, but I'm certain you're great with them. I'm sure all the boys have crushes on you, too."

She smirked. "Hardly. They're too focused on dreaming up excuses about why they didn't do their homework."

He studied her intently, totally oblivious to the crowd milling around them. "Pardon me for saying this, but I can't see you as a high school teacher. You're just so nice. Don't they take advantage of you?"

"Sure they do. Every year I have to set boundaries in the beginning. What about you? Is it fun being an editor?"

"It is! I love helping writers perfect their work, and I'm extremely gifted at spotting factual errors, always suggesting better ways of communicating ideas."

"You're so humble," she joked.

"I'm good at what I do," he stated simply.

"Do you get along with your coworkers?" She wanted to know everything about him. He intrigued her.

"Yes, I do. I work with some very talented journalists. And most of them are outgoing and friendly."

"Most of them?"

"Sure. There are a few introverts who keep to themselves. One guy is shy *and* introverted, so I'm afraid to even glance his way. Anytime I have to ask him something, he has that deer-in-the-headlights look."

They began walking again, this time slowly passing the shark tank. She briefly wondered if they could burst through the glass and eat her.

"Maybe he has a crush on you."

Dax shook his head. "Nah, I don't think he dates men or women. He has three cats and is the nerdy, homebody type."

"That's cool."

The two had a great time that afternoon, staying for almost three hours. They exited the aquarium, the cool air a refreshing change after being indoors where everyone coughed and sneezed around them. One man had come up behind Patience and coughed on her shoulder. By the looks of him, she could have sworn he had the flu. Immediately she'd prayed for protection from his sick germs.

Dax held her hand as they strolled to his car. Before she knew it, he stopped abruptly in the middle of the parking lot, pulled her body against his, and kissed her softly. A truck honked, going around them and speeding away, but they paid no attention. Dax and Patience were in their own tiny world, his arms around her waist and her hands on either side of his face. The kiss lasted only a few seconds. As they parted, their eyes locked, and she knew she was smitten. A family of four passed by, and the preteen pointed at them, exclaiming, "Eww!"

Neither said a word. They silently made their way to his car and got in. Dax turned to her, opening his mouth to speak, yet no words came out. Patience felt warm inside, but not from the heater. The kiss had curled her toes. She stared at the dashboard, unable to meet his gaze. She could almost hear her parents and friends warning that this was too soon. She agreed. However, she didn't regret the time spent with him. They got along so well and had fun being together.

The ride home seemed to take forever because of the awkward silence. The radio played country music, his favorite, and she stared out the window, her mind racing.

What am I doing? I just got out of a relationship, but here I am kissing a new guy. Am I crazy? This can't happen. I need to mourn Jonathan.

"Patience," he began as he pulled into her driveway, "I hope you're okay with what just happened. Believe me, it wasn't planned. I knew you didn't want to rush things, and now I'm scared I blew it. I'm sorry."

"You're fine. I didn't exactly resist your kiss, you know."

"So we're good?"

"Yes." She smiled sincerely, her hand on the door handle. "Thanks again for the fun afternoon."

He started to get out, but she stopped him.

"Don't worry about walking me to the door. It's okay." She didn't trust herself. The temptation to invite him inside was huge. The sooner they parted, the better.

He frowned. "I want to make sure you get in safely."

"I'll be fine."

She leaned over to give him a quick hug, the butterflies in her stomach fluttering wildly. She heard him mumble something about having a good time, as well. She exited the car, and in a flash, she was inside her house. Rory greeted her instantly, jumping up on her legs with enthusiasm, but all Patience could do was stand there in a daze. Her lips were still tingly from his kiss. She closed her eyes and could see Dax perfectly. She found it hard to believe that a guy who looked like him also had a great personality and undeniable charm. And even though she'd sworn off men just two weeks before, deep down she hoped he called her soon.

Chapter 23

The first week of February came with unseasonably warm temperatures. Patience sat across from Dax in the food court at the mall, her attention switching from all the activity around them to Dax as he talked about his friends. For the life of her, she didn't know how he'd talked her into going out with him again. More important, she couldn't figure out how they'd ended up at the mall. First of all, the weather was too nice to be indoors. They both wore shorts and T-shirts. Secondly, she hated shopping. It was at the top of her list of things to avoid if at all possible.

She took a bite of ice cream, trying to focus on what he said. But instinctively, her mind wandered back to the day they'd gone to the aquarium. Dax had called her late that night, apologizing profusely for kissing her and promising to be a gentleman from then on. She'd told him that friendship was all she had to offer. To her surprise, he'd accepted, saying he was willing to be friends rather than nothing at all.

Jana was the only one who knew about him. Patience didn't have the heart to tell her parents or Cole. It didn't make sense to her, so she couldn't expect anyone else to understand the predicament. Thankfully, Jana hadn't lectured her. All she said was that she didn't approve of rebound romances and to be careful.

"I know what you're thinking," Dax said, bringing her back to the present. "But I swear I only have one more store to go to, and then we'll leave."

"You're so sweet. Don't worry about it. I'm actually having fun."

He reached across the table to touch her hand. "*You're* the sweet one. You don't like shopping, and yet here you are, suffering in silence. You're awesome."

She waved a hand dismissively, blushing under his intense gaze. Every time he looked at her, she swore he could see every pore in her face.

"The only reason I agreed was to help you pick out an anniversary gift for your parents."

Rolling his eyes, he muttered, "And the only reason I'm getting them something is because I'm their son. Plus, I don't want my extended family thinking I'm an ass for not having a gift for them."

She locked eyes with him. "You see? Its comments like that that make me wonder about your relationship with them. Can you elaborate, please?"

A group of teenage boys passed their table, and all eyes were on Patience.

"Wow, she's hot!" one of them said loudly.

Dax nodded. "She sure is."

He leaned forward, propping his elbows on the table for support, and kissed her. For a brief moment, she was offended. Only six days before, she'd insisted on friendship. However, she hadn't pulled away from him this time, either. The attraction

206

between the two was more powerful than either of them. So she really couldn't blame him.

Returning to his seat, he exhaled deeply. "I'm so sorry."

She jumped to her feet, gathering the trash and pulling her purse over her shoulder. Avoiding eye contact, she motioned for him to follow her.

"We better get going if you have another stop to make." She tried to sound nonchalant, but her voice shook slightly.

"Patience, we probably need to talk about this." He grabbed the shopping bags and fell into step beside her, pausing briefly to dump the trash.

She shrugged. "There's nothing to say. We obviously can't keep our lips off each other." A passerby heard her and giggled.

Dax smiled. "You're crazy. We'll continue this conversation in the privacy of my home."

* * *

Dax lived in a huge, one-bedroom apartment in Plano. Ironically, his place was just ten minutes away from Jonathan's house. God definitely had a sense of humor. Feelings of guilt and sadness returned as she stepped into his living room. She came very close to feigning sudden illness, insisting he take her home. It would've been only a partial fib, as she was a bit nauseous.

"Would you like something to drink?" he asked, standing so close to her their bodies almost touched.

A beer sounds good, she almost said. She wanted something to take the edge off, yet she didn't need anything clouding her judgment, especially since they were alone. Their attraction toward one another was growing by the minute.

"A glass of water would be great."

She sat on the couch and waited, her heart pounding in her chest from anxiety. She took in her surroundings, impressed by how his apartment was decorated. She wasn't surprised by the eccentric style he'd used, with many different shades of browns and greens splattered throughout his living room. The black leather couch had leopard-print throw pillows, and there were contemporary floor lamps and unusual paintings on the walls. She noticed small safari animal statues on the coffee table, and a stack of *Reader's Digest* magazines lay on the end table.

"Here you go," he said cheerfully, handing her the drink before turning the stereo on. Jason Aldean's "Don't You Wanna Stay" filled the air, and Patience smiled.

"You really do like country music, don't you?

"Yes ma'am. What about you?" He sat next to her, close enough to twirl a lock of her hair with his finger as she talked.

"Some country music is fine, and I also like alternative and hip-hop."

His finger grazed her shoulder, creating tiny goose bumps on her arms.

"Do you want to know what else I like?" His voice was husky.

"What?" she whispered, the butterflies returning to her tummy.

"I like being with you."

Warning bells went off in her head. She liked him, too. More than she cared to admit. She liked everything she knew about him so far. But she needed more time. This couldn't happen. Not yet. She wished she could shrink him and put him on her nightstand to save for later, after an acceptable period of time had passed for her to respect Jonathan.

He scooted closer to her. Summoning all her strength, she got up and stood in front of a huge painting on the wall.

"Ah, *The Kiss*. I love this painting. Gustav Klimt is one of my favorite nineteenth-century artists. I critiqued some of his work for one of my classes in college."

Although her back was to him, she could hear Dax approach her, and in the next second, she felt his breath on the back of her neck.

"Look at me," he said, and she turned to face him, taken aback by his serious expression. He placed his hands on her shoulders.

"You want to be cautious, so you're keeping me at arm's length. Your ex must have hurt you badly. I don't blame you for being scared. I've been burned in the past, as well. It makes you believe it's better to push everyone away rather than risk heartbreak again."

She didn't move. It took her a moment to realize she was holding her breath. Exhaling loudly, she waited for him to continue. She noticed the color of his eyes had darkened to near-purple again.

He continued. "That said, I don't believe in bad timing when it comes to meeting special people. It doesn't matter if someone ended a relationship recently or hasn't dated in years. Anytime you get involved with someone, you risk getting hurt." He shrugged. "So the important thing is not *when* you meet but that God put you and the other person in the same room at the same time."

Again she said nothing.

He smiled. "Oh, and chemistry. It matters if you have chemistry."

Silence.

He ran a hand through his blond hair, causing it to be even more spiked than before. "Look, I'm not going to pressure you. But as I said before, I'm direct. And I have to make sure you know how crazy I am about you. I don't want fear to be the cause of us missing out on something magical."

He walked over to turn the stereo off. They could hear a fire truck's siren as it raced down the street. Patience returned to the couch wondering what to do next. What Dax said made sense, but she did think rushing into another relationship so quickly was foolish, at least for her. People did it all the time, yet she wasn't like everyone else.

Dax sat beside her. He took a sip of water and appeared to be deep in thought.

As she studied his features, all common sense flew out the window.

"I'm glad God put us in church on New Year's Eve. You're right. There is a reason our paths crossed," she said softly.

He nodded, relief written on his face. "There is an undeniable spark between us. I'm so happy you feel the same way." He reached for her, and with one hand behind her head, he gently pulled her to him for a long, passionate kiss.

Chapter 24

On Valentine's Day, Dax surprised Patience with a romantic dinner at Three Forks, an upscale restaurant in Dallas. He'd made reservations a little over a month in advance, claiming he'd known they would be dating when he'd first met her. She sat across from him at their table for two in the Lafayette Room, which was impressive with its fifteen-foot ceilings and huge chandeliers. The hand-painted murals added charm to the elegant room, while the fireplace gave it a cozy feeling. A vase filled with a dozen long-stemmed roses sat on their tiny table near the window. Dax had surprised her by having the waiter bring them out when he'd taken their orders. The centerpiece was a taper candle, its light casting a romantic glow between them.

She glanced out the glass window into the Burnett Room, her eyes misty from emotion. She was the type to cry at the drop of a hat, especially when someone did something so thoughtful for her. Couples filled both rooms, and servers were bustling around, weaving their way between tables while balancing heavy trays on their shoulders. She noticed a man who appeared to be in his early twenties kneeling in front of his date, a tiny velvet box in his hand. The young lady's hand flew to her mouth, which was hanging open, and in the next second she was nodding, throwing her arms around him, and crying. Love was definitely in the air at Three Forks.

Swallowing the lump in her throat, she turned her attention back to the guy of her dreams, who waited expectantly for a response.

Grinning broadly, she said, "You knew we'd be a couple by now, huh?"

He took a bite of his lobster tail, chewing slowly as he watched her. Self-consciously, she bit her lower lip, drumming her fingers on the table. She sat up straighter in the chair, adjusting and readjusting the low neckline of her tight, black dress. Finally, in an effort to relax, she rested her elbows on their table, forgetting that her plate of vegetable ravioli was teetering close to the edge. She jumped as her plate flipped over, bottom-side up, on her lap. Ravioli and snap peas slid down her dress, the green sauce extremely hot, as it had just come out of the oven.

"Ouch!" she exclaimed, scooting back quickly in her chair with wide eyes. Dax stood and was by her side in an instant, using one hand to rake the scalding food off of her and the other to signal to their waiter. Patience stood as well, reaching past him to grab a cloth napkin, her forearm knocking over the vase filled with roses. Water spread at rapidly, trickling down the sides of the table onto the restaurant's plush carpeting. The people seated near them turned to stare, and one woman smiled sympathetically. The waiter arrived with a busboy, so Patience backed up a bit to get out of their way, her bottom bumping into the table. Hard.

As if in slow motion, the candles wobbled back and forth before collapsing, setting the tablecloth on fire.

"*Oh no!*" she shrieked as the bright orange and red flames grew, and she and the busboy put them out with towels from his cart. Similar to the fire, her cheeks burned. She was mortified beyond belief. Her heart thundered. All she could do was continue to help clean the mess, praying the floor would open up and swallow her. She glanced at Dax, who was smiling at her. She couldn't believe how confident he looked, as if they were still sitting and chatting about nothing. Tucking a curl behind her ear, she rolled her eyes, carefully kneeling down to pick up stray ravioli.

"I can't believe you're laughing at me," Patience hissed as they climbed into Dax's car.

"I can't believe you tried to kill us all on Valentine's Day!" He burst into fits of laughter, backing the vehicle out of the tight parking space. He was parked way too close to an F150 and had narrowly missed scraping the truck's door with the front end of his Lexus when they'd arrived. She had held her breath when he squeezed into the spot against her wishes, acting as if he hadn't seen the available spaces that were farther away from the entrance.

She giggled. "Well, I can't believe everyone gawked at us! Haven't they ever seen someone spill food and set a tablecloth on fire before?"

He put the car in Park at a four-way stop, unbuckled his seat belt, and leaned over to cup her chin in his hand. He looked deep into her eyes, his expression suddenly serious.

"I can't believe I'm lucky enough to be in the presence of such a warm, gentle, klutzy, and beautiful woman," he whispered. "There is no other person in the *world* I'd rather spend this special night with." He kissed her, his hand on the back of her neck and his fingers entwined in her hair. His tongue found its way inside her mouth, and she sighed, scooting her body as close as she could to his in the bucket seats. She reached up to touch his smooth cheek, taking one finger to softly trace his jawline. He pulled back slightly, just long enough to make eye contact and whisper her name.

His lips met hers again. This kiss contained more passion than the first, his mouth devouring every part of hers, for there was a sense of urgency as he tried to show her how he truly felt. She inhaled deeply, arching her back and sighing contentedly at his touch. He moaned, his hand traveling slowly to the front of her neck, then her shoulder, and finally resting on her breast.

"Dax," she whispered.

Suddenly a loud *honk* came from behind them. They had forgotten their surroundings and the fact that he was parked at a four-way stop near the restaurant.

"Dammit," he muttered, buckling his seat belt again. She giggled and he glanced at her with a wink before putting the car in Drive.

"To be continued," he promised.

* * *

"Here we are," Patience said with a shy smile. She and Dax sat in her driveway for a while chatting. She looked down at her dress, the green sauce visible even on the black fabric at night. She couldn't care less. This was probably the only night she would wear it, anyway. Tomorrow it was back to jeans and a T-shirt.

"Sorry your car smells like ravioli."

He reached up to give her hair a playful tug. "That's okay. Just make sure that next time, its coffee you spill all over yourself. I love the aroma of Starbucks!"

"Deal!" She paused a second, then leaned over to give him a quick peck on the cheek. "Thank you for a lovely evening. You're wonderful."

His face fell. "You're not going to invite me in?"

She hesitated, unsure of what to do. She wanted to spend more time with him but didn't trust herself. Things had heated up pretty quickly earlier, and she wasn't quite ready to take it further. She wondered why he had to be so amazingly attractive, so charming and perfect. It made him hard to resist. Yet she had to. For her own sanity.

"I think we better call it a night," she answered cautiously.

"But Rory misses me," he whined, sticking his lower lip out and pouting.

She grabbed her purse and the roses, fighting the urge to set everything down and climb onto his lap for another make-out session.

"Patience, please let me come in. I promise I'll behave."

"But will I?" she asked with a smirk, only half joking.

"Mmm," he replied, reaching for her hand in the dark. "You're driving me insane." Kissing the back of her hand, he sighed dramatically. "Now that I think about it, you're right. It's best if I go home. I'll call you when I get in."

Frowning, she got out of the car. Disappointment filled her as she made her way to the front door. She already missed him.

With one last wave, she let herself in, tripping over Rory and almost dropping the vase in the process. She groaned, realizing she'd forgotten to give Dax his gift, Tim McGraw's latest CD. She had also written him a poem for their special day, whipping it up in less than twenty minutes. Once she'd pulled the laptop out, settling in on her sofa the night before, the words had come so easily. She couldn't wait for him to read it.

Heading toward the bathroom, Patience knew she had made the right decision by sending him home. The lust she felt for him had her on pins and needles. It was like a monster just ready to burst out of her and attack him. And while she had ignored the fact that it was too soon for a relationship, agreeing to begin dating him, it was way too soon for sex. She paused at the doorway, shivering slightly as she remembered their intense kisses. She definitely needed a shower, an ice-cold one.

Chapter 25

By the beginning of March, Patience and Dax were inseparable. Almost every free moment they had was spent together. They loved going to the Dallas Aquarium, the bookstore, and to the movies. And now that warmer weather had arrived, they were able to go hiking and camping. They went for long walks in the evenings, sometimes taking Rory along, which he loved. Most of all, they enjoyed doing low-key activities such as hanging out at coffee shops and spending time alone at home. They couldn't get enough of each other, always having great conversations and finding out something new about the other.

The two had even gone dancing with Jana and her new boyfriend, Bryce. She couldn't believe her best friend was willing to meet Dax, considering she didn't approve of the relationship. However, after double-dating, Jana begrudgingly admitted that he was a dream. Like Patience, she couldn't resist his charm and outgoing, friendly personality.

"Just be careful," Jana had warned for the hundredth time.

And for the hundredth time, Patience had ignored the advice. If her friend uttered those words once more, she would pull all her curls out. She was sick of hearing it. She and Dax had been dating long enough to be in the safety zone, which meant that she felt totally at ease. They both had let their guards down, and she decided to follow her heart this time, trusting her instincts instead of worrying herself sick about everything. It was ridiculous to put a timetable on mourning a previous boyfriend. This was why Jana was the only one who knew about him. Patience didn't feel like being lectured by her parents or Cole for jumping into a new romance.

* * *

The second Saturday in March, Dax's cousins, Blake and Shelton, threw a house party and told him to bring Patience. She asked him what she should wear, and he was clueless, so she settled for a sexy red top and jeans, figuring it was a compromise of casual and dressy. She straightened her hair, which hung past her shoulders, and wore minimal makeup. From the expression on his face when he picked her up at seven, he approved. She thought his eyes were going to literally pop out of their sockets.

The two stood in her foyer with Rory running circles around them. Dax wrapped his arms around her waist, pulling her against him aggressively, a sly grin on his lips. She threw her arms around his neck, and he kissed her lightly on the tip of her nose.

"You look too yummy for this party. I think we should stay here tonight," he cooed, his breath warm in her ear.

"We should go."

He kissed her hard on the mouth.

"On second thought, maybe we shouldn't go," she purred, her insides turning to mush.

He groaned. "Let's hurry and get there so we can leave early."

* * *

The party was thrown at Blake's three-bedroom house in Carrollton. His brother, Shelton, answered the door, his face breaking into a huge grin at the sight of them.

"Come in, come in," he welcomed, grabbing his cousin's wrist and practically dragging him inside. It wasn't until a moment had passed that Shelton focused on Patience, who was standing behind Dax, and his jaw dropped.

"Whoa! Who do we have here?"

Dax laughed. "This is my girlfriend, Patience."

Shelton took her hand and kissed it, a seductive smile on his handsome face. She could see the family resemblance, although Shelton was short and had dark hair and eyes. He also looked a lot younger, but she'd learned from Dax that he was actually twenty-two. She was sure his boyish features and height gave him the ability to pass for sixteen. She giggled.

"It's nice to meet you."

He chuckled. "Believe me, the pleasure's all mine."

Dax took a step forward, taking her hand out of his cousin's grasp and throwing his arm around her shoulders protectively. "As I said, this is *my* girlfriend."

Shelton shook his head. "Yet another example of why life isn't fair. Come on, follow me and I'll get you two something to drink."

They weaved their way through the crowd to the kitchen

where Blake was taking hors d'oeuvres out of the oven. He looked up when they entered.

"Hey!" Blake took off the oven mitt and shook Dax's hand, pulling him toward him for a quick hug. "We're so glad you could make it!" Catching sight of Patience, he released his cousin to greet her.

"Hi, I'm Blake. You must be Patience." Smiling sincerely, he hugged her.

"It's so good to finally meet you," she said. "Thanks for inviting me."

He winked, turning to Dax. "Man, you weren't exaggerating. She really is drop dead gorgeous!"

She blushed and Shelton nodded. "For once, I agree with him. Does she have an identical twin I could hang out with?"

Dax threw up his hands. "Will you two please stop? You're giving me a complex. I'm taking her home right now before someone steals her from me!"

"Aww, our poor little cousin's feeling insecure," Blake teased. Unlike Shelton, he looked nothing like the others, his red hair and pale skin a striking contrast. He offered Patience a beer, and fifteen minutes later, she and Dax were mingling with some of their friends. They had to shout to hear what each was saying, and at one point, he took her hand and led her to the patio for some fresh air. The temperature was slightly cooler than before, and she snuggled closer to him as they sat on the porch swing.

"This is nice," she said, gazing up at the star-filled sky.

"Yes, it is. Of course, you make everything nice. We could be trapped in shark-infested waters and I wouldn't mind, as long as we were together."

"That is so corny."

"Thanks," he said sarcastically, bringing his lips to hers.

"Mmm," she murmured, twisting her body toward his and placing her hand softly on his cheek. His hand went around her waist as he kissed her eyelid, then her nose, and then her chin. He was a great kisser, and her body responded to his touch immediately. She felt his lips travel downward to her neck, where he began to gently nuzzle and bite. She didn't care that they were at a rowdy party where, at any moment, someone could come out and catch them. Actually, that added to the thrill, and she could have stayed there forever.

"Dax, I really like you," she said suddenly, running her hands through his short hair.

Pulling back slightly, he stared into her eyes. "You're so wonderful. I really like you, too. You're all I think about." His hand was on her thigh, and he gave it a gentle squeeze, sending shivers throughout her body.

She melted into his arms, and before long, they were making out heavily. She was sitting on his lap, facing him, her legs dangling over the sides of the swing as she caressed his neck and shoulders while they kissed. He ran his hands through her curls, and then slowly they moved over her neck and chest, pausing to squeeze her breasts, and she heard him moan, which turned her on even more. He reached around to grab her bottom, pulling her up higher on his lap, and she bit his lower lip hungrily, wanting him so much, right then and there.

"Dax," she said again, reaching under his shirt.

Suddenly a group of guys burst through the patio door, stopping in their tracks as they got an eyeful of the lusty scene. Patience jumped up, her face flushed, and Dax quickly pulled his shirt down, standing next to her like a deer caught in the head-lights. The guys just laughed and continued on their way, jumping in the pool seconds later, fully clothed. Shaking her head, she laughed, turning to Dax and wrapping her arms around his waist.

"I was ashamed at first, but then I remembered that everyone here is probably either drunk or making out as well!"

He chuckled. "You're right about that!" He pressed his body into hers. "So shall we hop on the swing and continue?"

She shook her head. "No way!"

"I was joking! Come on, let's go back inside and dance. But if anyone hits on you, I'm beating him down!"

* * *

It was three a.m. when Dax brought Patience home. They had a great time at the party, and before they left, Blake and Shelton had invited them to a cookout they were having the following weekend. They'd promised to come, and she made a mental note to bring a dessert. She adored his cousins and couldn't wait to hang out with them again.

As they pulled up to her house, she noticed Cole's car parked in the driveway. Dax parked next to the curb, his brows furrowed in concern.

"Who is that?"

Cole got out of his car, leaning against the door with his arms folded across his chest.

"That's my best friend, Cole." She opened the door, but not before hearing Dax exclaim, "Your best friend is a *guy*?"

Dax and Patience walked up the driveway, and she wobbled

a bit. She'd consumed three beers throughout the night, and she was a lightweight.

"Coley, what are you doing here at this hour?"

He didn't answer. Instead, he eyed Dax suspiciously.

"Oh! Cole, this is Dax, my, um . . ."

Dax raised an eyebrow, his hands in his jeans pockets.

"Your what?" her best friend asked, his dark eyes appearing almost black from his mood.

"My boyfriend." Her shoulders sagged as she studied the ground.

Dax extended a hand to him, and surprisingly, Cole shook it.

"Hey, man, good to meet you," Dax mumbled.

"Yeah," Cole responded.

"Well, I guess I'll go," Dax said abruptly, turning on his heel and heading to his car. Patience followed, unsure of what to say.

"Call me when you get home," she said, but he didn't turn around or answer. She watched as his taillights disappeared down the street, and then she returned to her friend, who glared at her in the darkness. They faced each other silently, and she wondered how she could explain why she'd hidden her new romance from him.

"I'm sorry," she began, but he held up a hand to stop her.

"Don't bother. I just came over to make sure you were okay. I hadn't heard from you in a while, and I've been calling you all evening and night. I was worried."

Her heart plummeted to her feet. "Thank you so much for checking on me." She tried to smile. "I couldn't ask for a better friend."

He nodded. "We *are* friends, and I thought we told each other everything." He looked so hurt she almost cried.

Taking a step closer to him, she reached out to touch his arm. "Please understand. The only reason I kept this from you was because I knew you'd be worried. Everyone kept warning me that it was too soon to jump in a relationship."

"It is."

"See? I wanted to make my own decision and not have you or my parents talk me out of dating him."

He shrugged, flinging open his car door with force. "Oh well, it's your life. Just don't come crying to me when he hurts you."

"He won't. He's a great guy. It's hard to explain, but we have this connection. Actually, we're kindred spirits."

"You're so credulous," he said, shaking his head as he turned the ignition.

"What does that mean?"

He laughed. "Ah, the irony of your question astounds me! It means, my dear friend, that you're gullible, unworldly . . . "

"Cole!"

Putting the car in Reverse, he looked at her with pity. "Hey, I'm just calling it like I see it. Good luck with Dave."

"His name is Dax!" she called out in frustration as he backed out of the driveway. Patience stayed there for a moment, all alone in the dark, fuming inside. Cole made her so mad sometimes, acting as if he knew more than she did about life. She couldn't stand it when he treated her like a kid. She wanted to throw something, but there was nothing lying around except tiny rocks, so she stomped her foot instead. She turned on her heel, a smile tugging at her lips. Maybe she did act childish sometimes.

Chapter 26

"Will you please stop apologizing? Baby, it's okay. We're good," Dax reassured. He kissed her lightly on her forehead.

Patience frowned, sitting back in the passenger seat of Dax's car and trying to relax. It was Sunday afternoon, and they were five minutes away from Studio Movie Grill, a theater where people could eat and watch a movie simultaneously. Thankfully, she was able to pick the movie this time, and she chose a comedy. She needed a good laugh, especially after the tense moment with Cole the night before. After he had left, she'd tried several times to call Dax, but he wouldn't answer. Finally, she'd texted *just wanted to make sure you got home okay* before climbing into bed. When he texted back *yes*, she'd felt relief mixed with disappointment. One-word responses usually meant the person was upset.

And yet, when he picked her up for their date, he was in great spirits. It had almost made her nervous. She didn't want him to be offended or angry about the awkward encounter earlier, but his perkiness caught her off guard. She glanced at his profile out of the corner of her eye as he pulled into a parking space, and he appeared to be in a great mood. The lot was packed, and once again, he'd gotten way too close to a Chevrolet Suburban. She gasped.

"Why in the world do you park so close to big trucks?"

Smiling, he took his seat belt off and leaned toward her. "I love getting a wild reaction out of you."

His lips met hers in a tender kiss.

She smiled. "Okay, I'm going to stop overreacting."

Taking her hand in his, Dax gazed into her eyes. "You can do whatever you want."

Ashamed, she looked out the window. "You're right. I hesitated before introducing you as my boyfriend last night, and you're fine with it."

He placed his hand on her chin to make her look at him. "It upset me at first, but when I got home, I realized there must have been a good reason for it. So I let it go."

"I knew Cole would give me hell for dating someone new so soon. He can be overprotective at times. Jana was worried, as well, but she got over it. She really likes you."

"What about your parents? When do you think they'll be ready to meet me?"

His question surprised her.

"You want to meet them?"

He grinned. "Of course I do! I mean, in my opinion we're getting pretty serious. Naturally I would like to introduce myself so we can all get to know each other."

"Wow! That's awesome! I know they would adore you," she said, giving his hand a gentle squeeze, her cheeks beginning to ache from smiling so much. She couldn't suppress it. She was excited to show him off to her parents.

Suddenly he glanced at his watch. "Crap! We're late for the movie. I'd forgotten where we were."

He jumped out of the car and ran around to her side to open the door for her. Patience expected him to take her hand and pull her toward the entrance. He hated being late. Instead, Dax leaned against the car and grabbed her by the waist, pulling her close to him. His blue eyes glistened with mischief. He kissed her hard on the mouth, and she sighed happily. He definitely wasn't against public displays of affection.

* * *

The next Saturday afternoon, Patience and Dax were in the bakery department at the grocery store. All week she had been looking forward to Blake and Shelton's cookout. They were hilarious and fun to be around. And as a bonus, it gave her another opportunity to be with Dax. She wished she could spend every waking hour with him. The past two and a half months had been nothing less than a dream, as far as she was concerned. She was falling for him, and there was nothing she could do to slow it down or stop it.

"Will you please just *pick* something? We're already thirty minutes late," he said in exasperation.

"There's no rule that says we have to be on time for a barbecue," she replied. "Besides, if you would've reminded me last night about the dessert, I could have baked something then."

He chuckled, picking up a container of brownies. "Don't put this on me. I don't know why you waited until we were a blink away from their house to say something."

She rolled her eyes. "It doesn't matter. Will you please go

get some chips or something so I can shop in peace? Besides, Shelton doesn't like chocolate, so put those down."

"How do you know he doesn't?"

"He told me at the party. You were in the restroom. Now go!" She pointed toward the other aisles, and he swatted her bottom playfully.

"Okay, babe. Meet me at the self-checkout in three minutes. I'll miss you," he said tenderly, and she smiled. He was such a sweet guy, always telling her exactly how he felt at any given moment. She was a lucky girl.

"All right, sweet pea," she cooed. "I'll miss you, too."

Patience wandered around the bakery in search of the perfect dessert to take. She'd wanted to take something homemade to impress them. She wanted them to know she had taken time to out of her day to bake for their cookout. Shrugging, she decided to get a grip. It wasn't that important. She could tell they liked her, and the feeling was mutual. Plus, Dax was probably pacing near the front, anxious to get out of there.

She picked up a tray of white chocolate chip cookies and started to head up the aisle when, suddenly, she froze. Standing a few feet away from her next to the bread was Pete, the manager of the furniture store she'd gone to many months before. He bent down to get a bag of muffins, and as he stood, he turned to face her. They locked eyes. Her heart began to pound ferociously in her chest, and her palms were moist with sweat. She took a step backward, trying to tell herself she was overreacting. He was just a racist stranger. His blue eyes narrowed behind his glasses.

Deciding to shrug it off, she began walking past him toward the front of the store just as Dax rounded the corner.

"Babe! Did you decide to bake the dessert after all? What's taking so long?" He took a closer look at her and reached out his hand. "What's wrong?"

She shook her head, continuing up the aisle. "Everything's fine. Let's just go."

He started to follow and then stopped when he caught a glimpse of Pete.

"Dad?"

Pete approached them quickly, his eyes never leaving Patience.

"Dax, what are you doing here? I thought you were at work."

"I don't work on Saturdays," he answered with a frown.

She couldn't believe her ears. Pete was his *father*. This had to be some cruel joke. She stood watching the two with her mouth hanging open.

"Who is this you're with?"

"Her name is Patience, and she's my girlfriend," he answered proudly, putting a protective arm around her shoulders, his chin held high.

The bag of muffins fell to the floor, but instead of picking them up, his dad stood looming over them, clenching and unclenching his hands tightly. His blue eyes darkened right before them, appearing almost purple. She noticed instantly the resemblance between father and son, although Dax had blond hair and wasn't as muscular as Pete. Yet the biggest difference was that Dax had a kinder-looking face and an aura of warmth that surrounded him. Anyone would feel comfortable approaching him.

"Excuse me, I don't think I heard you correctly," Pete said, his voice raised an octave. A middle-aged woman at the deli counter turned to stare.

"What is your problem?" Dax asked irritably.

"You know exactly what my problem is," his father hissed through clenched teeth. "We'll talk about this later." He stormed past them, nearly knocking a passerby down as he bumped into her.

"Hey, watch where you're going!" the woman commanded loudly.

Pete kept walking, leaving the muffins on the floor and his son in a huff.

Dax turned to face her. "Sorry about that," he began, but Patience headed up the aisle as well, her curly hair flying behind her.

"Babe, wait up!" he called, breaking into a sprint to catch up. She quickly went through the self-checkout lane, paying for the cookies while ignoring him.

"What is it? I mean, I know my dad was rude, but you don't have to punish me for it." He stood next to her while she yanked the receipt out of the machine so hard it ripped down the middle. She started to walk away, but he took hold of her wrist, a smile tugging his lips.

"Sweetie, we're not moving an inch until you tell me what's bothering you."

"Let me go."

He pulled her closer. The cashier for the express lane stopped to watch with an amused look. There were no customers in her line.

"I won't, not until I find out what's up."

"Your dad ..."

232

He smiled. "He's an ass. I already know. Both my mom and dad are idiots." He leaned forward, rubbing his nose with hers. "That's why I can't stand them." He laughed, trying to lighten the mood.

She pulled her arm out of his grasp. "Let's just get out of here, okay?" Attempting to smile, she sneered instead.

"You have to kiss me first."

The cashier chuckled.

Patience shrugged. "Fine," she said, leaning forward and giving him a peck on the cheek.

Shaking his head, he grinned mischievously. "I don't think so." He put his hands on her shoulders and kissed her lovingly.

"Aww," the cashier sighed, and a few customers laughed.

Chapter 27

Patience was subdued at the cookout, her thoughts on Pete and Dax. Memories of that warm August night when he'd refused to do business with her came flooding back like a tidal wave. She couldn't believe that eight months later, she would run into him again. What's worse, she had fallen for his son, who happened to be a wonderful person. What luck. She wondered if God was angry with her for something she did and was punishing her. This was the craziest thing ever.

"Hello, earth to Patience," Blake said, waving a hand in front of her. The two were sitting in lawn chairs by the pool, waiting on Dax and Chris to return from the convenience store. Chris was Blake's neighbor, a guy in his early twenties who lived with a roommate. He had volunteered to go on a beer run when more guests than expected had showed up. He asked Dax and Patience to go with him, but she'd declined, offering to help Blake instead. The boys had gone without her, and Dax had resembled a wounded puppy when he'd kissed her good bye.

"I'm so sorry! What were you saying?" She took a sip of her water and tried to focus on him.

"I was just asking if you are okay. You seemed distracted."

"I'm fine." She watched as their friends lounged around

them, some bobbing their heads to the music while drinking and laughing, and others had brought swimsuits and were wading in the pool. Everyone was in high spirits, cracking jokes and basically enjoying the warm weather. Blake and Shelton had some great friends. They had been so nice to her, including her in their conversations and trying to get to know her better. And of course, two guys had waited until Dax was gone to hit on her.

Blake ran a hand through his red hair. "I don't know about that. You were a million miles away just now."

"It's no big deal. I really am okay."

"All right, but I'm a great listener. If you ever need to talk, I'm here."

He was such a nice guy. She was touched by how thoughtful he was to her. And she could tell that he meant it. Dax was blessed to have such great cousins. She understood why they were so close. All three of them were good people.

She reached over to touch his arm. "Thank you. I'll remember that." She changed the subject, however, refusing to ruin his barbecue with her downer attitude.

* * *

Dax muted the television, his full attention on Patience as they sat on Blake's couch. It was early evening, and while most of the guests had gone, a few still lingered out back. Shelton was in the den with a girl he had a crush on, and Blake chatted with the others outside. Patience sighed heavily, trying her best to perk up. She snuggled in closer to him, getting a whiff of his aftershave, and she closed her eyes.

"Mmm, this is nice," he whispered, wrapping his arms tightly around her. "I can't get close enough to you."

"I feel the same way."

He kissed the top of her head, and she felt him shiver when she nuzzled his neck softly.

"Thank you for bringing me to the cookout. I had a great time. And I love your cousins!"

"They love you, too! And I believe Blake *really* likes you. Normally I'd be jealous, but he's harmless."

She giggled. "You're so confident." She pulled back slightly to gaze up at him. "I like a man with a healthy dose of self-esteem."

He kissed her lips tenderly. "Patience," he started.

"Yes?"

"I . . . like you."

"I like you, too." Her heart began to race.

"I mean I like you, you know, a lot."

Their eyes met for a long moment, and she knew what he meant.

"I can't believe we've known each other only three months," she said, amazed at how connected they were spiritually and emotionally.

Dax nodded. "You're the only girl I've ever felt this way about."

Her arms tightened around his waist, and she kissed him once more before laying her head on his chest. They stayed that way for a long time, with him reclined on the couch and her body pressed against his, holding each other in their tiny world.

Chapter 28

"I have to ask you something," Patience said, taking Dax's hand in hers and kissing him lightly on the forehead. They stood on her parents' front porch the next day, both of them still wearing their church attire from that morning. It had been a great service. The message was about forgiveness, and the preacher had spoken out of Matthew. Patience always felt so serene and peaceful when she went to church. She was glad Dax had suggested they go.

"What is it, babe?" He looked handsome and a bit nervous in his navy blue shirt and black slacks, his skin a tad darker from all the time they had spent outdoors lately. She thought it wasn't possible for him to get any better looking, but he had.

"Well," she began tentatively, "would you mind terribly if I introduced you as my friend, just for now? My parents won't understand why I have a boyfriend so soon after my ex."

Guilt soared through her as his expression changed from hopeful to annoyed.

"This is only for a short while," she quickly added, "until they get to know you."

He withdrew his hand from her grasp, taking a step backward. "I know what this is all about," he said, folding his arms over his chest. "You're ashamed of me. That's why you hesitated last night when I brought up meeting them."

He raised an eyebrow. "It's because I'm white, isn't it?"

"*What?*" she shrieked. "No, that's not it at all!"

He threw up his hands. "I don't believe you. What else could it be? I'm not too young or old, I have a good job, and I'm not ugly."

She laughed. "You're a nut, that's what you are! Baby, how could I be afraid because of your race when my dad is white?"

"Excuse me?"

"I'm mixed, goofball!"

He took a step toward her. "You are? I just assumed you were black."

Grinning broadly, she reached over to grab his waist and pull him against her.

"My dad is white, my mom is black, and they're both going to fall in love with you, Dax. I'm sorry if I hurt your feelings. I wanted them to meet you with an open mind. I want to spend the afternoon getting acquainted, not defending our relationship."

He nodded. "All right, I'll do this for you. But promise me you'll tell them the truth about us soon."

"I promise."

* * *

By the end of the day, John and Sharise McKlendon were crazy about Dax. He wowed them with his good humor and charm, just as he had with Jana. It also helped that he loved sports and outdoor activities. He and her father had clicked instantly,

240

excusing themselves after lunch and retreating to the den. She could hear them chatting about camping, fishing, and their favorite football teams. She helped her mom clean the kitchen, and then they joined the men to play video games and Wii Sports.

They had a great time, and Patience yawned as they climbed into her car with one last wave to her parents.

"Okay, your mom and dad are awesome!" He started to kiss her and then stopped, his blue eyes wide. "Oops! I almost made out with you right here, and they're on the porch."

He fastened his seat belt.

She giggled. "That would not be good, *friend*." Putting the car in Drive, she slowly pulled away from the curb. She glanced over at him, a mischievous look in her eyes. "Just wait until I get you alone, though."

Chapter 29

The following week went by fast. The kids in Patience's classes cooperated, paying attention during her lectures and turning in homework on time. It was an episode straight out of *The Twilight Zone*, but she didn't question it, for fear she would jinx everything. On Wednesday night, she met Jana at the gym, and she worked on her novel Thursday evening, completing five chapters. She tried calling Cole a couple of times that week, but he didn't answer, nor did he respond to her texts. She knew his silence was her fault, but she couldn't apologize if he didn't pick up the phone.

"Maybe he likes you as more than a friend," Dax suggested on Friday night. They'd chosen to stay in and relax, so he'd rented a movie and snuggled with her on the couch. Rory was staying with her parents for the night. Sharise had called earlier that day complaining that she missed him and needed a Rory fix.

"You sound like my mother."

"She's a smart woman."

She shrugged. "Nah, we're buddies. He treats me like a kid sister."

He twirled a lock of her hair, looking pensive. "I don't think so. The fact that he waited in your driveway until three a.m. for you, asking all those questions and giving me the evil eye makes me wonder."

"He was worried about me."

"He was jealous."

"No, he was not."

"Okay, well, then I am!"

She reached over him to get the remote, hastily pushing the Pause button without taking her eyes off of him. Something about his tone made her take him seriously.

"I thought you didn't get jealous."

He ran a hand through his hair. "I didn't think I would feel threatened by him, but I do. The way he looked at you. I don't know. I could just tell. He has feelings for you."

Patience touched his cheek softly yet said nothing.

"You two have a history. You share childhood memories and have this bond. I can't compete with that. And it doesn't make me feel any better that he's handsome."

She watched as his eyes clouded, turning that purplish-blue color she liked so much, her heart about to burst from the deep emotion she felt. It took a lot of courage for him to reveal his insecurities, and she appreciated the gesture. He resembled a small child, innocent and vulnerable that night.

"You don't have to compete with him. I'm yours," she assured, her voice faint even in the quiet living room.

His gaze never wavered. "I love you, Patience."

He didn't wait for a reply. His lips met hers in the dimly lit room, and she responded, kissing him with an intensity that almost frightened her. She slowly reclined on the couch, gently pulling him down with her. She moaned, her desire for him growing more and more as she ran her fingers through his hair.

"Patience," he whispered, his lips nuzzling her neck hungrily and his hands beginning to explore her body. She closed her eyes and lost herself in the moment, arching her back as his hand went under her blouse. She inhaled deeply, holding her breath for a second and then releasing it slowly.

"I love your scent," she murmured, rubbing his back before letting her hands travel down to his rear, giving it a firm squeeze.

"Babe," he whimpered softly in her ear as he buried his nose in her hair.

"Oh, Daxy." She rocked her hips and knew there was no turning back. This was the night she would give herself to him, body and soul.

"I love you, too."

Chapter 30

"I love you," Dax said for the tenth time that hour, lightly running his finger up and down Patience's back.

Shelton rolled his eyes dramatically. "Oh my word, will you give it a rest? She knows you love her, okay? We all do!" He jumped up from his lawn chair and went to the cooler, snatching a bottle of beer and snapping the cap off immediately. He chugged a quarter of it and then stomped back over to them.

Blake, Chris and his girlfriend, and three others shook their heads while Patience adjusted her swimsuit strap. The sun shone brightly on them that first weekend of April. Everyone was overjoyed because of the hot weather, and she already had a slight tan from jogging with Rory. Dax said she was even yummier with darker skin, and she just giggled. Their skin tones almost matched, and he constantly held his arm next to hers to compare. He got a kick out of it.

Turning on his mushiest voice, he gave her a peck on the cheek. "I love, love, love you, my sweet angel! You're all I think about morning, noon, and night," he cooed loudly, and Shelton made gagging noises.

She was probably the only one who felt sympathetic toward Shelton, who had broken up with his girlfriend only the week before. He'd caught her cheating on him with one of her friends, and he was devastated. According to Blake, he had fallen pretty hard for her. This experience had altered his outlook on women and relationships, and he claimed that no one could be trusted.

"I need to cool off," Shelton said, and seconds later, he jumped in the pool. Chris and his girlfriend joined him, and Patience smiled.

"Baby, you really shouldn't tease him like that. Take it easy. He's heartbroken. Let's not rub our happiness in his face."

"Why should I hold back because of him? He'll be in a sour mood whether we are lovey-dovey or not. Please!"

Everyone laughed, and they all sat around basking in the sun and talking. Blake got up to flip the burgers on the grill, and their friend Jimmy went inside for more bags of Doritos. Bob Marley's music played in the background, and when Jimmy returned, he decided to take a dip in the pool as well. Dax and Patience shared a lawn chair, and the others were sitting at the umbrella table.

There was a lull in the conversation. Blake turned his attention to Patience.

"So, Dax says he met your parents last weekend. That's awesome!"

She nodded, unable to suppress a huge grin. "Yep, and of course they fell for him instantly. We had a great time."

"Things are moving pretty fast for you two lovebirds, huh?"

Dax smiled. "It is so weird how time flies. In a way, it seems like I just met her yesterday because I still get nervous and excited when I see her." He shrugged. "But then again, we're extremely comfortable around each other, like we grew up together or something."

"That is so sweet!" a girl named Karen piped up. "I wish there were more romantic guys out there like you." The other girl nodded in agreement.

Blake took a drink of his soda. "Have you met Pete and Dana yet?"

She felt Dax stiffen beside her, and his arm tightened around her shoulders. "She hasn't yet. Well, we ran into Dad at the grocery but ..."

"Ha! How did *that* go?" his cousin asked, clearly amused.

Patience began to perspire, but not from the heat. She tried to block the image of Pete's scowling face from her mind. She could think of a million other subjects she'd rather talk about than Mr. Whites Only.

She hesitated. "It went well."

"Don't lie. My father was downright rude, but we'll give him another chance. How about we invite ourselves over to their house one evening next week? As a matter of fact, let's plan on it. It's time for you to meet them."

She almost threw up on his lap. There was no way anyone would make her go to his parents' house, even at gunpoint. She would much rather be trapped in a room full of mice or kidnapped. She had to think of a good excuse and quick.

Blake burst into laughter. "You should see your face right now! Your eyes are about to pop out of your head! I can't say I blame ya. Uncle Pete is a monster to everyone he comes in contact with. Aunt Dana's a little more pleasant, if you like cruel, ruthless people."

"Oh my!" Karen exclaimed, rising from her seat. "I'd hate to be in your shoes, Patience. Good luck," she called, turning on her heel and running to dive into the pool.

Dax stood to stretch, reaching his arms toward the sky with a frown. The sight of his Tweety Bird swim trunks should have lightened the mood, but it didn't.

He nodded. "Blake's right. My parents are horrible. But regardless of that fact, I'm introducing you to them next week, if for no other reason than to get it over with."

She kept her mouth shut, her mind racing as she tried to think of a believable excuse for never, ever going over there. She couldn't believe both parents were nightmares. Poor Dax!

"You have my condolences," Shelton said as he returned to the group. "I couldn't help but overhear, and I have to say that it was nice knowing you."

Ignoring his cousins, Dax grabbed two burgers and opened them up. "Do you want lettuce and pickles, sweetheart?"

She nodded, her mouth suddenly dry.

"So, how about Monday night? We can go have a quick dinner with them, and then we'll have the rest of the week to relax."

She grimaced. "I think I have a conference with one of the parents that evening."

He sat next to her, balancing their paper plates carefully. "Tuesday?"

"No good, I'm meeting Jana for a girls' night out."

He smiled. "That's not a problem. We can head over there on Wednesday. I'll call Mom and set everything up."

Silence.

Patience picked at her burger, pulling the bun apart into tiny pieces and rolling them into balls. "I'm working on my book that night."

Blake, Shelton, and Chris exchanged knowing glances. Dax cleared his throat.

"Let's try this differently. Honey, when would be a good time for you to meet them?" He popped a chip into his mouth and waited.

She smirked. "July might work."

Everyone laughed except Dax. She felt bad but had to be honest with him. It was time to fess up. "Baby, that afternoon at the grocery store wasn't the first time I'd met your father."

One could've heard a pin drop as all activity ceased. Blake leaned forward, resting his elbows on the table. He had forgotten to buy sunscreen, and now his pale skin was almost the color of his hair. Shelton didn't blink. Chris's girlfriend sat still as a statue, while Chris had started to take a drink but, instead, his cup remained suspended in mid-air. Karen stood near the pool, her head cocked to the side and a sympathetic smile on her lips.

Dax swallowed his food, his eyes narrowing as he studied his girlfriend's face. "What are you talking about?"

She stood abruptly, wrapping a towel around her hips. "Maybe we can go inside where there's a bit more privacy."

For a minute, it looked as if he was going to stay put. She held her breath. She didn't want to have this conversation in front of their friends. Finally, he put his plate down, allowing her to take his hand and lead him inside. They sat on the love seat facing each other.

"What is going on?" he asked, his body tense and his expression grim.

She opened her mouth, but nothing came out. Clearing her throat, she focused on the fireplace, trying to figure out what to say. With her hands clasped together in front of her, Patience told Dax about the night she had gone into Pete's Furniture and his father had refused to do business with her. She filled him in on everything, and when she finished, he was positively livid.

"Tell me this is an April fool's prank," he croaked, rising to his feet quickly. He strode to the other side of the room, his back to her. Her heart ached for him, but it was a relief to get this off her chest. Ever since she'd found out Pete was his father, a constant game of tug of war went on inside her. She'd kept waiting for the right moment, the perfect opportunity, to tell him about the incident but realized today that there never would be.

Wiping her damp palms on the towel, she sat on the couch, her wet hair a mass of tangles framing her lovely face. She would sit there forever, if need be, to give him time to digest the news. Out of the corner of her eye, she noticed a person's shadow on the carpet near the patio door. She looked up and saw that it was Shelton peeking in, and all she could do was shake her head. He was a trip.

After what seemed an eternity, Dax turned to face her. His tanned cheeks had changed to bright red, and his eyes were violet. His lips were pressed into a thin, tight line, causing tiny wrinkles around the edges. Hesitantly she stood and approached him. His arms went around her, holding on so tightly it took her breath away. It was as if part of him wanted to shield her from harm while another part was afraid he would lose her if he let go.

They clung to each other, and she kissed his hair, for his face was buried between her neck and shoulder. Closing her eyes, she inhaled his scent, which was void of cologne after swimming. She loved the way he smelled, the way he looked, and the way he made her feel. She was in love with his soul.

It took all her strength to pull away from him. She knew the others would come in soon, especially Blake, whose sunburn needed prompt attention, and Shelton, who was dying to stick his nose in their business.

Dax exhaled loudly, looking forlorn and somewhat lost. "Patience, I am so sorry this happened to you. I am thoroughly disgusted by my father's actions. I just can't wrap my mind around it. I don't know what to say."

"You don't have to say anything. And I'm sorry, but I had to tell you."

He hugged her. "Of course you did! I wish it had been sooner, like at the grocery store."

She rolled her eyes. "Are you insane? What was I supposed to do? Pick up the muffins and say, 'Don't bother introducing us. We met before when he discriminated against me at his store'?"

"Yes!" He cracked a smile, and she relaxed slightly.

Suddenly the patio door flew open. Their friends bounced in expectantly, with Shelton leading the way, and they surrounded Dax and Patience like a pack of hungry paparazzi waiting for breaking news.

"Well," Shelton broke the silence, "what did you two decide?"

Chapter 31

Dax and Patience were quiet on the drive home later that night. Neither one wanted to discuss Pete, nor did they want to chat about the weather. It suited her just fine. She was happy to look out the window while listening to sports radio. To be honest, there was nothing either could say to make things better. Dax had a father who happened to be prejudiced. End of story. Now all she had to do was figure out how that affected their relationship. Obviously they wouldn't be invited to any family reunions.

As if reading her mind, he glanced over at her as they entered his neighborhood.

"Babe, I hope you know that I don't share the same views as my father. I couldn't be more different from him if we were strangers."

"Dax! How can you even *say* something like that? Of course I know!" She shook her head. "I am so in love with you. It doesn't matter who your relatives are."

He reached over to grab her hand. "Don't get mad, but I still think you need to meet them."

"What?"

"Just hear me out." He pulled into his apartment complex

and parked. "Sooner or later you're going to bump into my parents. I mean, I plan on us being a couple for a while, and there will be events that force us to spend time with them, whether we want to or not. Family gatherings, birthday parties, and Christmas are prime examples of this. Remember when you helped me shop for their anniversary? Well, I didn't go to the party. I sent the gift with Blake and rented movies that night. My grandparents were furious, and so was my aunt." He shrugged. "My mom's sister cannot stand Dad, but she toughs it out. There's something about making an appearance, ya know?"

She shivered. "I get what you're saying. One of my uncles is a racist, and I have some cousins who get on my nerves. Yet I have to see them a couple of times a year, and I grin and bear it."

"Yep! That's why there are so many funny cards at Christmastime that talk about the horror of having to get together with loved ones."

She giggled, reaching over to stroke his cheek. "So true."

They kissed, and then she raised an eyebrow, their surroundings finally dawning on her. "Wait a minute! What are we doing here? I thought you were taking me home."

He nuzzled her neck, murmuring, "You and I have had a stressful day. You're spending the night with me so we can recuperate."

* * *

"Yes, Mom, we will be there by six. Okay, I'll see you this evening." Dax pushed End on his phone with an exasperated sigh. "Ugh! I can't stand it when she won't let me go! Next time I'll just text her."

Patience laughed nervously. They had woken up early the next morning so she could rush home and feed Rory. She'd cooked breakfast for them and then they'd gone to church, where she'd prayed heavily for herself, Dax, and Pete. She couldn't believe she had agreed to have dinner with his parents that night. He definitely had a way with words, convincing her that they needed to seize the moment and get the introductions over with. She did agree because she didn't want it hanging over her head indefinitely. It was time. She hoped they didn't put poison in her food, though.

"I think you hypnotized me," she whined on the way to the Christians'. She gazed at her reflection in the passenger mirror, wondering what they would think of her. She wore a simple white sundress with sandals, and her hair fell loosely around her shoulders. She'd thought about straightening it but decided not to. That was too much trouble to go through for them.

"How did you know?" he asked in mock seriousness, his eyebrows raised.

"There's no other explanation." Her stomach felt queasy as they pulled into his parents' driveway. "I think I changed my mind. Please take me home."

He turned off the car and wrapped his arms around her. "Sweetie, don't be afraid. I'll be with you. Oh, and heads up! I am talking to my dad about the incident at his store. I'll pull him aside after they've gotten to know you. But honestly, I have a pretty good feeling about today. Things will go well. And if not, we can leave. Now come on, let's do this."

Dax walked around to her side and opened the door, and they walked hand in hand toward the two-story house.

Before they could knock, the door swung open, and they jumped. A middle-aged woman with long blonde hair stood in front of them, and she immediately stepped onto the doorstep and took her son in her arms. Patience smiled as she watched his face, looking as if he had just eaten something distasteful. His mother was short and curvy, and she wore a low-cut dress and high heels. She had on quite a bit of makeup, and Patience guessed she was a pretty woman beneath it all.

"It's about time you came to visit! I haven't seen you in months," she scolded.

"Sorry, Mom," he responded in a flat voice. His eyes brightened when he turned to Patience. "Mom, there's someone I'd like you to meet."

Dana Christian's smile faded. She looked at Patience, her eyes traveling slowly from the top of her head to her feet. Patience squared her shoulders and held her head high.

"Hello, it's nice to meet you," Patience said, extending a hand to her. His mother accepted it.

"Hmm," was all she said in response. The three stood there awkwardly for a moment, with mother and girlfriend sizing each other up. It was Patience who broke the silence.

"Thank you for inviting me over this evening."

Mrs. Christian nodded toward her son. "You can thank Dax. It was his idea." Her green eyes had turned cold, and Patience shifted her weight from one foot to the other.

"Gotcha," was the only response she could think of. His mom flipped her hair over one shoulder.

Taking another stab at small talk, Patience smiled. "I've

heard so many good things about you." She prayed God would forgive her for the lie, especially since they had just attended church that morning.

"That's funny. I haven't heard a thing about you. As a matter of fact, Pete and I didn't know our son was dating anyone."

"Mother!" he cut in.

"Well, it's true. You hid her well."

Patience bristled. This woman exuded no warmth or charm as her son did. Instead, there was an aura of arrogance and superiority that hung over her like an invisible cloud. She glared at the woman who had raised Dax, not caring if she noticed. She didn't want to be rude, but she was tired of being extremely nice and patient with people like Mrs. Christian. It had brought her nothing but headaches in the past, and it was time to fight back.

"Let's go inside," Dax hissed.

Dana went in first, and Dax reached for Patience's hand, but she ignored him. They followed his mom into the expansive living room, where they found Pete watching television. Her stomach turned over at the sight of him. He looked up, gave a quick nod, and then turned his attention back to the show.

"Dad, we have company." When Pete didn't acknowledge them, he stormed over to grab the remote, turning off the TV and standing by the couch.

His father threw up his hands and got up to go to the mini bar, choosing a bottle of Scotch from the wide variety of alcoholic beverages. They waited as he poured himself a shot in a tiny glass and proceeded to consume it in one gulp. Then he looked at Patience, focusing on her forehead.

"Welcome to our home," he said, resembling a bad actor reading his lines from a script.

She frowned. "Thank you."

"Well, let's eat," his mother said dryly, leading them into the dining room.

Fifteen minutes later, the four sat around the table with little to say and zero appetite.

"So," Dana turned to Patience. "Tell us about yourself."

"I'm a teacher who enjoys watching football, reading, going to the movies, and spending time with my family," she answered in monotone.

"Do you work at a daycare?"

"No, I don't."

Dana picked up her glass of wine. "Preschool?"

"No, I teach high school English."

Her eyes widened. "*You* have a college degree. I'm impressed."

Dax cleared his throat. "Uh, Mom, I can't believe you cooked! And it's edible. Write this down on your calendars, folks!"

Patience sat up straighter. "Believe it or not, my entire family made it past the third grade." She knew she was being defensive and paranoid but couldn't help it.

"I didn't mean-"

"I know what you meant."

Pete jumped in. "When did you and my son start dating? Where did you meet?" They could tell he didn't really care and just wanted to steer the conversation in a different direction.

"We met at my church's New Year's Eve celebration." She

took a fork and poked holes in her steak, which she had no intentions of eating.

"Oh, really? What religion are you?"

"Baptist."

His father took a bite of potatoes, chewing thoughtfully. "Ah, that makes sense."

Patience set her fork down. "What does?"

"The fact that you're Baptist. Most of your, er, kind are."

"I beg your pardon. My church has members of all different races."

Pete picked up his glass, noticed it was empty, and then stood for a refill. He shrugged. "I meant as a whole."

He turned to leave the room, but her next question stopped him.

"Do *you* go to church?"

"Uh, well, no, I ..." he stuttered.

"Ah, that makes sense."

Dax jumped up. "Babe, can I talk to you for a minute?" Not waiting for an answer, he pulled her chair away from the table. Caught off guard, she almost fell to the floor. Dana sat with her mouth hanging open, and Pete stayed rooted to the spot, his face beet-red.

Dax practically dragged Patience by the wrist into the study, shutting the double doors behind them.

Before he could say anything, she pointed an accusatory finger at him. "This is all your fault. You knew your parents would eat me alive but insisted on having this stupid dinner."

"Look, it hasn't been that bad. All they've asked is what you do for a living and where you go to church. Let's go back in there and give it one more try. It'll get better."

"I didn't realize your mother was a bigot, as well. I thought it was just Pete," she hissed.

His eyes widened. "She's not a bigot. She just has these pre-conceived notions about certain ethnicities." He tried to laugh it off. "I guess she watches the news way too much."

She wondered if he was trying to convince himself more than her. "No, I will not spend another minute fighting against their narrow-mindedness and rude comments."

He moved closer, wrapping his arms around her. "Please do this for me. They don't know what to say, is all. I never bring women to meet them. There has not been anyone important enough to take this risk, the risk of having someone believe I'm like them, because I'm not. You're the first one, honestly. I know it's difficult for you to believe, but they're nervous. They will loosen up once they get comfortable. I want them to fall in love with the Patience I love. It won't take long for them to see how intelligent, warm, and sweet you are. Please, baby," he finished, his eyes pleading.

"Fine," she said irritably. "But one more insult and I'm outta here."

Dana was clearing the table, and Pete was in the living room when they returned. Dax and Patience joined him, sitting on the love seat across from the couch. The three of them watched television until his mother came in and sat next to her husband. Patience decided to zone out, brainstorming different ideas for her novel.

"Mom, did you know Patience does volunteer work, too? That's something you guys have in common."

"That's nice, dear."

"Yeah, she donates her time to one of the shelters for pregnant teens. She assists with the parenting workshops where they teach them different things like parenting skills, giving advice and basically lending an ear to those who are scared or depressed. It's pretty awesome."

Pete scoffed. "If you ask me, all those girls need is a swift kick in the rear. If they'd have kept their legs crossed like they had good sense, they wouldn't be in that predicament. And whatever happened to birth control? Now people like me have to pay for their carelessness. My tax dollars support them."

Patience rolled her eyes. "On the contrary, those women need compassion and support. Anyone knows that birth control isn't one hundred percent. Once they find themselves in this position, the last thing they should have to face is a person who is closed-minded and judgmental. That just causes the women to shut down or become defensive and agile. It's a shame how some people in society treat others based on their limited knowledge of a situation."

Dana set her wine glass down.

"How many children do you have?"

"None."

"Really? How old are you?"

"Twenty-five," she answered in exasperation, silently telling herself to keep an open mind about the questioning.

"Don't take this the wrong way, but you're the first young woman of color I've met who doesn't have children."

That was it. Patience had had enough. She stood, her arms folded across her chest. "Could you be more specific, please?" Her voice dripped with sarcasm. "Did you mean white, peach, or brown- colored women?"

Everyone froze, and she charged toward the foyer. Just

then, there was breaking news on the television. A young Hispanic male had just robbed a bank in Dallas. The suspect was still at large, and witnesses told police he was armed and dangerous.

"I'm not surprised," Pete muttered. "Mexicans will steal anything not bolted down with a chain and lock."

Patience whipped around, her green eyes flashing. "You could have at least waited until I left the room before making that racist comment! How dare you!"

He stood quickly, glowering at her. "I didn't say *your* people steal."

"Yeah, well, I won't tolerate your hateful opinions about any minority. There's no telling what you say about black people!"

"You need to calm down, girl!"

"Who are you calling girl?"

To her surprise, Dax was at her side in five seconds.

"She's right. I tried giving you and Mom the benefit of the doubt, always making excuses to everyone for your bigotry. And stupid me, I thought if you met Patience, you would see that there are good people in every race." He cocked his head to the side, looking contemplative. "You know, I don't think you two have ever had a minority in this house. All you do is turn on the news and focus on a few criminals, and then you jump all over it, insisting that the entire group is bad."

Dana remained on the sofa, her fourth glass of wine now empty in her hand.

"Mom, Dad, you two have been nothing less than cruel since we arrived. I'm ashamed to admit you're my parents."

"You watch your mouth, ya hear?" his father yelled, taking a few steps toward them.

"The truth hurts, doesn't it?" Dax said as he slid an arm around her waist.

"I am not a racist!"

"What else would you call someone who refuses to wait on a customer just because she's black?" Patience could see that everything was finally getting to Dax, who had remained so calm up until this point. His volume almost matched his father's. "You're an asshole as well as a racist pig!"

As if in slow motion, Pete lunged at his son, slapping him hard across the face. Both women screamed, and in the next instant, Dax grabbed hold of Pete's collar, trying to pull him down. His father was solid muscle, especially in comparison to Dax's thin frame, so he was only successful at ripping his shirt. This fanned the flames of his dad's anger, and he effortlessly pushed Dax to the carpet and straddled him. Dax reached up and yanked his dad's eyeglasses off his face, tossing them across the room.

"You little weasel! If anyone should be ashamed, it's me! How did I end up with a pansy for a son?"

Dana screamed again, bending over the two and wrapping her arms around her husband's neck, grunting as she tried to pull him off of her child. It was no use. Neither she nor Patience was strong enough to break up the fight. They watched in horror as Pete's hands went around his son's throat. He wiggled and squirmed, trying to break free, tugging at his father's arms in desperation.

"Get off of him!" Patience shouted. *"I'm calling the police!"* Dax's face was a frightening shade of red from gasping for air.

Either the sight of his son in a vulnerable state or the threat of the cops being called caused Pete to relent. He loosened his grip and released him, lifting himself off of him but re-maining on the carpet. He just sat there with his head down and shoulders slumped. Very gingerly, Patience helped Dax up, tears burning her eyes as he coughed and sputtered. The young couple didn't wait for him to catch his breath or gather his thoughts. Without a word, they fled the Christians' house, anxious to escape the ordeal.

Chapter 32

Patience woke up with a start at three a.m. the next morning. She sat up in the bed drenched with sweat. Her heart raced, and one arm was out of her tank top. Her curly hair was a mass of tangles, and her mouth was extremely dry. Rory, who had fallen asleep with her, now lay by the window. She shook her head, squeezing her eyes tightly shut and then opening them again, as memories of the bad dream came flooding back.

In it, she wandered through a dark forest searching for a way out. Everywhere she turned, either a large animal, monster, or tree blocked her path. Up ahead, an orange-colored light shone brightly. She ran toward it, relieved to have found an exit. However, the light was actually from a burning cross. A group of hooded KKK members stood around it. She took a step backward, preparing to flee, but someone grabbed her from behind, covering her mouth and leading her to the men.

"I found another one!" he yelled. The head of the clan approached.

"Excellent work," he snarled. He removed his red hood, and Patience gasped. It was Pete! His dark blue eyes bored into hers.

"You know, she's actually kinda pretty," he said wickedly, reaching out to touch her chin.

She rolled out of bed totally exhausted. She must have screamed in her sleep, causing Rory to seek peace on the floor. She opened the blinds to check her yard for suspicious activity. Part of her expected to see a burning cross or skinheads attempting to break in her house. She shivered. She couldn't discern between reality and imagination. She wished she could call someone, but it was only three fifteen. Her parents would have answered, yet she didn't want to worry them. Jana never heard the phone when she slept, and Cole was the last person on earth she wanted to reach out to.

Patience began pacing, unable to wind down and get control of her emotions. Unshed tears threatened to fall as she picked up her cell. There was no way she could fall asleep between now and six o'clock, the time she usually awakened for work. With trembling hands, she dialed Dax's number. She hated to wake him and promised herself she would only let it ring twice.

"Babe!" he answered immediately. He sounded alert, as if he'd been up all night. "What in the world are you doing awake at this hour?"

She giggled, surprised that she could laugh at a time like this. But he had that effect on her. He always brought a smile to her face.

"I should be asking you the same thing."

He sighed. "I couldn't sleep, so I've been reading self-help books all night."

"Aww, poor baby. Yeah, my next book will be titled *Caught in the Middle: What It's Like Being a Mixed Girl*."

He whistled. "That title is way too long. What about *It Don't Matter If You're Black or White*?"

"Those are lyrics to Michael Jackson's song. I would be sued faster than you could say biracial."

"Oh, yeah, that's right. What are you doing up?"

"I had a nightmare that your father was going to kill me."

"Babe, that's terrible. He attempted to kill *me*, so maybe you were having sympathy dreams."

"Baby, what are we going to do? Our relationship can't survive this."

"It can and it will. I will disown my parents. There's no need to ever see them again. I have my own money. I'm independent. Our children won't care if they only have one set of grandparents."

"You're so funny. I wish it could be that simple. We'd move to either California or Minnesota, where I could concentrate on my writing and you would continue editing."

"Hold on a minute. Scratch that. You would model and I'd be your manager," he said.

"That sounds good. We'd be broke, but I'm not materialistic or anything, so money doesn't matter."

He chuckled. "We would be rich! Have you looked in the mirror lately?"

Patience and Dax chatted a long time. He told her stories about his childhood, and how his dad would forbid him from playing with kids of other races in his neighborhood. But he had been as stubborn then as he was now, always choosing friends based on their character and not the color of their skin. His mother was no help, usually siding with Pete. Oftentimes Dax would sneak out and hang at his friends' homes, especially in his teens.

She glanced at her alarm clock, amazed that it was five a.m. Time had flown by as usual when talking to him. She yawned, stretching her thin body across her bed. She prayed she didn't fall asleep. If she did, she would wake up late for work.

"Are you feeling better?" he asked.

"Yes, I am. You always perk me up," she said softly.

"You're going to be pooped today at work. I hope the kids don't take advantage of you."

"I'll be fine. I may nap this evening."

"Good. I'll call you tonight. I love you, Patience."

"I love you, too."

* * *

On Friday night, Dax showed up bearing gifts for Patience and Rory. In one hand, he held a huge gift bag containing various chew toys and dog biscuits. In the other hand there was a plain pink envelope. They were going out to dinner, but it was supposed to be a casual date. She racked her brain, wondering if she had missed something.

"What's the occasion, sweet guy?" she asked as he stepped inside. Upon further inspection, she noticed that he looked drained. There were dark circles under his eyes, and his face was pale.

He shrugged. "I love you, that's all."

Her heart melted. She watched him give Rory his treats, laughing at the way Dax's voice changed and he began cooing at the dog. She was so lucky to have a boyfriend who loved both her and Rory.

She led him into the living room, and she opened the card. It had a sweet message about being in love with her, and there was a gift card inside to their favorite bookstore.

"Dax! Thank you! You didn't have to do this," she said, leaning over to kiss him tenderly.

"I wanted to. You're my angel."

She tilted her head to one side. "Are you okay? You look tired."

"I'm all right. Mom called last night to apologize for the other day. We stayed on the phone forever."

"What about your dad?"

"I haven't heard from him."

She smiled sympathetically. "Give him time. He'll come around," she lied. Deep down, she knew Pete wouldn't be sorry for his actions. He appeared set in his ways.

A shadow crossed his face. "I don't care if he ever contacts me or not."

She reached over to grab his hand. "Of course you do. He's your father. You love him. I know it's been crazy lately but I bet you two have a bond."

"Let's just drop the subject, okay? No one understands what I'm going through. My parents have never been supportive of anything I've done. They're too self-absorbed to be proud of my accomplishments. They only focus on the things I do that they don't approve of." He ran a hand through his hair. "I don't want to talk about them anymore."

"We don't have to, baby. Just know I'm here if you ever change your mind."

271

His expression softened. "Thank you. I'm sorry if I'm a little uptight tonight." He kissed her hand. "Now, let's go eat. I'm starving."

* * *

Over the next few weeks, Dax was on edge and moody. Whenever the couple went out, he appeared lost in thought or became defensive when Patience commented on his behavior. He had lost some weight, as well, and she was worried. She knew the cause of his depression was his parents. In her opinion, even if someone didn't always get along with his or her family, he still loved them and craved their love in return.

By May, their relationship was strained. Patience found herself making excuses to cancel their plans, and Dax caught on quickly. Her blatant attempts to avoid him upset him even more.

She threw up her hands in frustration. "Look, I'm sorry. It's just that I feel like I'm walking on eggshells around you all the time. You won't talk about your dad, but when I try taking your mind off him, you withdraw into your own little world."

It was a gorgeous, sunny Saturday, and they sat on the patio of his apartment glaring at each other. The wind ruffled her curls, which were in a ponytail. She looked sixteen in her shorts and tank top. He could have passed for a teenager, as well. He wore jeans and a T-shirt, and his hair lay down this time, as it had been a while since his last haircut.

"Well, I'm sorry if I'm not always so happy and in a good mood for you. I'm so stressed out!"

"I don't expect you to always be perky! But you've been snapping at me a lot."

"My mom has been pressuring me this past week. She says that my dad won't talk to me until I do things his way."

She put her hands on her hips. "I know what that means. They've given you an ultimatum, huh? Dump me or never step foot in their house again."

He looked away and her heart sank. She knew it. Her greatest fear had materialized. He'd chosen his parents over her. It made sense, but she could have kicked herself for not ending things sooner. This experience sort of reminded her of her ex-boyfriend Tripp. He had loathed his mom and dad, reassuring her that he would never change his mind, and he would always want to be with her. But she'd broken up with him, her instincts telling her that family was more important. She hadn't wanted to cause division between a son and his parents.

She should have done the same in this situation. Somehow, though, she'd felt this was different, that their love was stronger than anyone or anything that threatened it. She had been wrong. And now she sat there looking foolish and gullible, just like Cole had said. She angrily brushed a tear off her cheek, refusing to cry in front of him. She was mad at Dax for not warning her earlier that his feelings were changing. But most of all, she was disappointed in herself for believing love conquered all.

"Well, have a good life," she said, brushing past him to gather her purse and keys.

"Patience, hold on a minute," he said. By the time he finished the sentence, she was already inside the apartment. She was glad she'd followed him back to his place. Now she

273

wouldn't have to endure a torturous ride home with him at the wheel.

He followed her outside, trying to grab her arm, but she was too fast. With lightning speed, she had the car door open, not once glancing up at him.

"Wait! I'm not done talking to you about this!"

She threw her purse in the car and then whipped around to face him. "Are you kidding me? When I said your parents must have given you an ultimatum, you were silent. Ever since I met them, you've been depressed and anxious, which is understandable. I've tried making the best of it, but do you know how upset *I've* been to know they hate me because I'm black? No, you don't. I can't change my skin color, nor do I want to. I'm proud of who I am. I refuse to jump through hoops for anyone!

"Pete and Dana are your family. They raised you. They love you and you love them, whether you admit it or not. I won't come between you three. But don't make this more difficult by chasing me through the parking lot. I am saying what you're too afraid to say. It's over."

His eyes widened, and she noticed that they were moist with tears. "Maybe we could work something out. Let's just go back inside and talk about it."

"There's nothing to say. I can't be friends with you because my feelings are too deep. It would hurt too much, especially if you started dating someone else. And you will eventually. Then our friendship would fade away, and I'd be sad all over again. It's best to make a clean break."

He sniffled, a sullen expression on his face. He looked like a child who had lost his puppy. "Please don't leave me."

As much as it killed her, she had to let him go. She would never forgive herself for causing so much strife in a family.

"Good bye, Dax."

Chapter 33

Patience sat in church the next morning holding back the tears. While the choir sang, she opened her Bible to the book of Joshua, skimming the first chapter. God told Joshua three times to be courageous, and she thought that was significant. She desperately needed to read and reread that part, for she was feeling extremely weak and hopeless. She closed her eyes, praying for God to bless her with inner strength. She hadn't slept a wink the night before. She'd tossed and turned, her thoughts on Dax and the breakup.

He had called once, leaving a long message about how much he already missed her and asking her to call him. She almost had at one point, going as far as dialing his number but then hanging up. She hadn't believed she would make it through the night. Her entire body ached as if she had the flu.

Just as the preacher took his place at the podium, Patience turned to find Dax making his way toward the empty space next to her. Her heart flip-flopped in her chest. She had forgotten that he attended this church. He sat down and looked straight ahead, immediately opening his Bible and paying close attention to the sermon. She did the same. Even sitting perfectly still, he was a distraction to her. They all stood for prayer, and

Dax reached for her hand. The electric current traveled up her arm just like it used to.

When the service was over, she had no idea what the message had been about. It was as if she had temporary amnesia. She walked out of the building in a daze, trying to remember where she had parked. Out of the corner of her eye, she saw Dax sprinting toward her. She decided to meet him halfway, knowing it was a bad idea. Maybe church had softened her.

"Hi," he said as he caught his breath.

"Hi."

"How are you?"

She smiled faintly. "I'm not doing very well. And you?"

"I'm a basket case. I haven't slept nor eaten."

She shook her head. "Wow, we are pitiful!"

He touched her arm. "Listen, I just want to apologize for all the heartache I've caused. You mean the world to me. The last thing I ever wanted to do was hurt you."

"I know. And I'm sorry for my part in all this. I really wish you nothing but the best. I truly hope you can patch things up with your folks."

He took a step closer. "I'm taking a huge risk asking, but would it be okay if I called you every now and then to check in?"

She nodded. "Sure, I'd like that."

He grinned. "Are you serious? I thought you would say no."

"It couldn't hurt to keep in touch."

Staying true to his word, Dax called Patience frequently to check on her. It was difficult at first to hear his voice and not get all mushy. Once, after a lengthy conversation about his grandparents and how wonderful they had been, she almost told him she loved him. They were his mom's parents and adored by many. They'd died tragically at the age of seventy. Their plane had crashed when they were on their way home to New York after visiting Texas.

"My grandparents were sweet, open-minded, and so loving to everyone." His voice caught, and he was quiet for a moment. Patience wished she could reach through her cell and hold him.

Clearing his throat, he continued. "Anyway, I have no idea how my mother turned out the way she did. She's nothing like them."

"I've seen it happen before. A nice couple has children who wind up being brats. And sometimes rude, obnoxious people have well-behaved kids." She shrugged. "There's no rhyme or reason to it."

"You're right. In your case, both the parents *and* the daughter are pretty amazing."

They stayed on the phone over an hour, and she ached for him when they hung up. The sound of his voice tugged at her heart. She could picture him perfectly, as if he were in front of her. As she climbed into bed that night, she prayed she had made the right decision to remain friends with him.

* * *

On June first, Patience celebrated her twenty-sixth birthday at her parents' home. Cole and Jana were there, of course. Also, a few friends from college, Kylie and Sasha, surprised her by coming. Her neighbor Ronny and two teachers who taught at Stonebrook came, as well. John McKlendon grilled burgers and steaks, while Sharise prepared an array of sides, including Watergate salad, one of her daughter's favorites. They also had two cakes. The white one was in the shape of the number two, and the chocolate was shaped like a six. She was touched by all the hard work her mother had put into the party. There were strawberry cupcakes and tons of chips, cookies, and fruit.

Sasha put her arm around Sharise. "My birthday is November second, and you're in charge of baking," she said seriously.

Sharise nodded. "Okay, remind me at the end of October and I'll be on it!"

They had a blast that afternoon. The McKlendons had a pool, and the guests were told to bring swimsuits. They had fun eating, swimming, and playing games like charades and Scrabble. Patience received a lot of great gifts, too. Movie tickets, gift cards, and money were given by most. But Cole went all out. He gave her a beautiful James Avery bracelet along with money and Lisa Scottoline's newest novel.

"Cole! You went overboard! I can't believe this. You're so wonderful! I'm getting choked up," she gushed. She held out her wrist, and he put it on her. "You're the best friend ever."

Everyone fell silent in the living room, waiting for his response.

"No, you're the best. I haven't been that supportive lately, and I'm sorry. I hurt your feelings, and I don't deserve a friend like you, to be honest. You're too good. You're an angel on earth, blessing all who are lucky enough to know you."

All the women sighed, including Jana, who didn't always get along with him. John smiled, and Patience blinked away tears. They hugged tightly. The guests discreetly left the room, leaving them alone.

"I really am sorry," he whispered in her hair, still holding her.

"It's okay. I'm the one who kept things from you and put you on the back burner quite a bit. But I will never take our friendship for granted again."

He kissed her forehead. "Don't worry about it. Friends should always take a backseat to love interests." He winked. "Now, let's go swim."

Chapter 34

Patience didn't get home until close to ten p.m. She had helped her parents clean up after the party. She turned onto her street and noticed Dax's Lexus in the driveway. Pulling up alongside the curb, she grabbed all of her gift bags and hopped out of the car, excited to see him. He hurriedly rushed down the driveway to meet her, taking her in his arms and lifting her up to twirl her around. She giggled, realizing how much she'd missed the feel of his arms around her waist. She buried her face in his neck, inhaling the familiar yet intoxicating scent of his cologne. She dropped the bags, hearing something break in one of them, but she didn't care.

They stood there holding each other for a while and then finally broke apart long enough to gather her things and go inside. He followed her to the couch, and she faced him expectantly, a huge grin on her face.

"Happy Birthday," he said softly.

"Thanks, Dax. I honestly don't remember telling you it was my birthday."

He smiled. "I asked your mom the first time I met her."

She laughed. "You are so sweet, in a crazy way!"

She watched as his blue eyes darkened.

"What's the matter?"

He took a deep breath, exhaling slowly as he took her hand.

"The past three weeks have been miserable for me. I have enjoyed being your friend, and yes, my parents and I have patched things up. We're still not the best of friends, nor do I want to be, but we've been civil toward each other. Actually, I still cannot stand them. They're awful people. But I haven't beaten either of them up or choked my dad, so we're good.

"Patience, I miss you so much. I think about you constantly. We belong together. I've known that since New Year's Eve, and since we've been apart, there's no doubt in my mind. We're soul mates. I am nothing without you. I was a fool to let you go. Please say you feel the same way."

She did. She loved him tremendously.

Reaching into his pocket, he pulled out a tiny velvet box. She gasped when he opened it. Inside was a beautiful engagement ring. It was white gold with blue sapphires all around the band and a round diamond in the center. It was absolutely gorgeous. She could barely see through her tears as he got down on one knee and placed the ring on her finger. He had tears in his eyes, as well.

"Will you marry me?"

"Yes, Dax, I will!"